The Placebo Effect

The Placebo Effect

A Multi-Narrative Horror/Thriller

Steve Wyffels

COPYRIGHT© March 2021.
All rights reserved.

"The Placebo Effect"
Written by Steve Wyffels.

Edited by Steve and Sara Wyffels.
Formatted by Steve Wyffels.
Cover By Steve and Sara Wyffels.

Amazon Kindle Direct Publishing.

All people, places, and events are fictional, any resemblance is coincidental.

No part of this book can be reproduced in any way without permission.

This is a work of fiction and is intended for a mature audience.

BOOK CONTENTS:

<u>Chapter ... Title ... Narrator ... Page</u>

Prologue ... "Tell the Story" ... Adam ... 1
1 ... "Time to Boogie" ... Seth ... 8
2 ... "You like Jell-O?" ... Seth ... 16
3 ... "My Little Sister Laura" ... Seth ... 24
4 ... "The Teddy Bear" ... Seth... 38
5 ... "Bullseye" ... Sean Lynch ... 50
6 ... "In the Dark" ... Seth ... 55
7 ... "The Secret" ... Arielle ... 66
Intermission ... "Chunky" ... Adam ... 71
8 ... "Easy Money" ... Sean Lynch ... 77
9 ... "Bear Claw" ... Seth ... 87
10 ... "Accusations" ... Arielle ... 106
11 ... "Kerflooey Leg" ... Seth ... 119
12 ... "Territorial Pissings" ... Sean Lynch ... 129
13 ... "Gut Instinct" ... Arielle ... 141
14 ... "The End" ... Seth ... 152
Epilogue ... "It's Cold Out" ... Adam ... 159

Prologue
"Tell the Story"
NARRATED BY ADAM
(Spring 2017)

"No... please don't!" she cried as two men dragged her out of the city. "Please... stop! I beg of you!" She pleaded for her life... but they wouldn't hear it.

They said she broke the law, even though she was a hero. "You can't do this to me!"

Her wrists and ankles were bound together. There was no use trying to escape. She thrashed her arms and legs as much as they would allow, trying to wiggle free, but to no avail.

They dragged her through the street containing a crowd of gawkers, then shoved her against a stake and tied her up with a thick rope. "Please let me go," she begged again, but nobody flinched. "I don't deserve this!"

She held firm onto her crucifix, watching the men tighten the ropes around her, squeezing her, taking her already faint breath away.

Then she trembled at the sight of a man,

carrying a torch. He looked at her, and she saw evil in his soul. He threw the torch down at her feet, lighting the pyre...

She looked at the crowd gawking back at her, waiting for her to burn. Their dark, evil eyes staring blankly at her, lacking any reasonable empathy.

"Please!" she shouted. Nobody cared.

The fire combusted and began to consume her. Flames reached the sky... smoke ascended into the breeze...

And she screamed...

* * *

"That's how Joan of Arc died," Eric proclaims with a cheese-grin.

"Nice story... freak," I retort and sit down. Eric snickers.

I watch the flames dance in the trees, then disappear in the shadows. If I listen carefully, I can hear kamikaze bugs getting fried in the fire. A buzz, and then a sizzle... naïve, little creatures they are.

Burning in fire... that must be the worst way to go, especially being trapped, with no way of escape. But these bugs are just stupid, they don't know any better.

What about those who lived in the 15th or 16th century? Like Joan? People accusing one another, end up bound to a pole and set on fire. How could anyone do that to another human being?

I think it's absurd that crowds would gather to watch executions. People getting kicks... gaping at helpless victims. Just the thought of it makes me tremble. I guess I'm morbid, my mind is twisted. But really... I know *your* mind is too. So please... don't kid yourself.

The logs start crackling and popping from being exposed to the elements a little too long. The sound is a nice distraction from myself.

Gazing up at the firmament, the stars seem to wink at me. Moonlight washes over us as the clouds run away. I take a deep breath, the air is cold and crisp, and very refreshing.

"Adam, think fast."

"Whoa!" I shout as a beer can nearly rips my face off. "Damn dude, easy."

"My bad," Eric says with a sneer on his face.

I walk over and pick up the can of beer. *Not going to open this just yet...*

I look at the fire again and ponder... so fascinating... so mysterious. The rising heat makes the sky look distorted. How is it that fire can cleanse so beautifully, yet destroy so permanently? What phase of matter is it considered anyway? Yeah, I know... they say *plasma*, but is it really? Think about it...

But whatever, no one cares.

I'm chilling with friends out in the woods, in a big field carved out in the middle... I think it used to be farmland but now it just sits here, literally growing weeds.

A bonfire and some beer, tents for later, it's all good. But I hate setting up tents, I can never seem to figure them out.

Crickets conduct a symphony all around us. Their constant chirping is relaxing. It gives me a sense of comfort, (when the critters go silent, you know something is lurking nearby).

I walk over to the hedgerow and pick up a log, then bring it over to the fire. "Time for the story ladies," I say with enthusiasm.

Everyone gathers around the fire. Tanya, Desiree, and I had carried lawn chairs over from my house. Matt and Eric decided to sit on logs. I told them I had more chairs, but they insisted the logs were good enough.

Matt's a super fat kid I met at work. He's a cool dude, but damn... put down the cheeseburgers! People pick on him because he waddles when he walks... he's so funny looking. But he doesn't care, he calls *himself* a lard-ass. He needs to invest in a treadmill or call Jenny Craig or something.

"Get me a beer," Matt demands.

"Get it yourself tubby, you need the exercise," Eric shoots back, looking around to see if anyone else finds him humorous.

And Tanya, well... she's the exact opposite. Probably four-foot-nine and ninety pounds soaking wet. She has jet-black hair that's always messy. I don't think she knows what a brush is. She likes to wear those jeans that can fit a person in each leg, and she wears chains and dog collars around her neck. But she's quirky and fun to hang out with... always cracking jokes, then laughing at them. She's the tomboy of the group, just one of the guys. You should hear her belch after chugging a bottle of Mountain Dew.

"Do I have to?" Matt asks, scrunching his face. He acts like making the walk to the cooler will be strenuous. He sucks in some air and lifts himself up. *That-a-boy...*

Desiree is a girl we know from down the street, who just likes to hang out with us. We aren't exactly sure why... she's way out of our league. She's super pretty with curly, blond hair and big, blue eyes that sparkle. She's more into typical girl things like doing her make-up and nails and wearing Abercrombie & Fitch.

Eric ran into her at the local Sunoco gas station one day, he *literally* knocked her over. He was in a big hurry and wasn't watching his steps. He apologized, and they had a good laugh about it.

He asked her what her name was, and she didn't run away. He held onto that moment like Elmira held onto Furball. He convinced her to come to my house later that evening. I don't know what kind of swag he put on, but it must have worked. I was introduced, and she's been part of the gang ever since.

"That's not how you do it!" Desiree blabs, mocking Eric for failing to turn over a burning log. She grabs a stick off the ground, then takes the stick out of his hand. "This is how it's done," she says, showing off.

Eric has been a friend of mine most of my life. He's tall and lanky, kind of awkward looking. But he's a cool guy. We're always getting into trouble... getting in dangerous situations for no reason. He likes to play *beer-pong* a lot... and he's pretty good at it.

"So, you gonna tell the story or what?" Tanya asks, waking me from my daydream.

"Get on with it already!" Desiree teases.

"Yeah... my bad," I say.

"What's it all about?" Tanya asks.

"I can't give the story away, you have to wait," I explain.

"That's not what I meant," she pauses. "I mean like, where did you hear it? Where did it come from? Eric says it's legendary."

"Oh. It's a... family story, passed down through the generations," I say flippantly, sipping my beer. "At least, that's what my mom says. I don't really know much about the rest of my family, my dad or my grandparents..." I put my head down. "I don't want to talk about it."

"Oh sorry, I didn't mean to..." Tanya starts.

"Don't worry about it," I say quickly, sipping my beer again. "Over the years, my mom has told the same, old story. She gathers anyone who will listen... serves drinks... makes popcorn with extra butter..."

"Nice!" Matt exclaims.

"And she would have a stern, serious look on her face," I continue. "One time, I could have sworn I saw her lip tremble..."

"That's weird... wouldn't that make you think she's hiding something?" Tanya speaks up.

Maybe Tanya should just shut her face...

"Well... it's probably just part of the act she puts on," I respond pointedly.

"Oh, *right*," Tanya chuckles.

"Who wants s'mores?" Matt asks, unzipping a bag full of goodies.

"I do!" both girls reply.

"Alright everyone... shut up and listen," Eric shouts.

You see, the thing is... when Mom *does* tell the story, it always seems so real. But I guess... maybe that's the point. I pull up my chair and begin...

One

"Time to Boogie"
NARRATED BY SETH
(Summer 1998)

"Great!" I shouted sarcastically... the red and blue lights flashing in my rear-view mirror. I lowered the pipe from my mouth. I had just left work, two minutes prior, and was racing home to get out of my nasty smelling clothes... like rotten fish and garbage. Not cool. Even after six months, my nose hadn't adjusted to the foul smell.

I opened the center console and tossed the pipe inside, trying not to let the cop see me moving around too much. I usually look for cops at that intersection, but it was dark outside, I didn't think anyone was watching.

I quickly lit a cigarette, trying to disperse the smell of weed. Again, not moving around too much... then he would ask questions, and I don't have time for that.

I pulled over and put my parents' minivan in park, clicked my blinker signaling right and waited patiently for the cop to approach me. The road had been freshly paved, and they had moved the shoulder over, which was necessary for such a busy highway. *And no more potholes...*

It was raining outside. Little drops of water on the back window made the red and blue lights look big and bright and all distorted.

After a few moments, the officer got out of his vehicle and walked up to my window. I had it rolled down about halfway.

"License and registration please," the officer said, beads of water bouncing off his hat.

"What did I do?" I asked coyly.

"You didn't stop at the sign," he said with a facial expression that shouted, *duh...*

"Oh..." I said and handed him my license.

The funny thing was, I hadn't even attempted to stop... I hadn't even slowed down. I blew through the stop sign, taking a right-hand turn, about as fast as I could...

"Where are you coming from?" he asked. "And what's that smell?"

"The cigarette or the fish?" I joked. He wasn't amused. "I just left work, the restaurant behind the mall over there," I answered, pointing over my shoulder. "I'm on my way home." The officer nodded his head, then he started shining his flashlight in my face. I had to squint and turn away. Then I reached for the glove box and opened it. "I know my registration is in here somewhere, just give me a sec."

I started to shuffle through papers and other junk, when a red and black pipe fell from its hiding place. "Damnit Jeff," I said under my breath. He must have forgotten it the last time we went on a burn cruise.

"What's that young man?" he asked, putting his spotlight right on it.

"What?" I pretended not to hear him.

"Okay, step out of the vehicle," he said sternly.

"You got to be kidding me," I mumbled. Then I saw my registration in the glovebox and quickly grabbed it. I reluctantly stepped out and walked over to Officer Smith. (I saw his badge.)

"Walk over here. Stand against the vehicle," he barked. "And put out that cigarette." I flicked my smoke on the ground, Officer Smith rolled his eyes. I walked over and faced the patrol car. He put a pair of handcuffs on me, then spun me around and told me not to move. Water was dripping off my nose and my chin.

"I was just trying to get home sir, I'm really not a bad kid," I said, trying to sound innocent and proper.

"Well, that's not going to happen just yet," he said without glancing at me.

"This is dumb," I spat, rolling my eyes. Other vehicles were speeding by, probably pointing and laughing at me as they passed.

"Yup, sure is," the officer replied with a chuckle. "When did you plan on renewing this registration?"

"Excuse me?" I asked.

"This expired last month!" he said with a weird look on his face. "Okay, let's go." He shoved me against the cop car, opened the door and said, "Get in."

What luck did I have? I still smelled like fish, and now I was in the back seat of a cop car that smelled like hooker sweat. Just nasty. The combination of smells from my clothes and the back seat vinyl made my nose hairs curl.

After a few moments, another squad car came rolling up. "Damn, it's not like I robbed a bank or anything," I told myself. I watched the other car come to a stop and a female officer stepped out. She had bright, red hair in a ponytail that looked transparent in the headlights. She was young... and pretty.

She approached Officer Smith and the two started talking. *Where have I seen her before? That cop, she's so good looking. She reminds me of someone else I know...*

Then the female officer's radio went off. I couldn't hear what was being said, but in the headlights, the look on her face was frantic. That's when Officer Smith quickly jumped back into his car. I was staring at the holes in the ceiling fabric

when he turned on the siren and punched the gas...
"Whoa," I gasped, surprised by how fast the squad car took off. "Where are you taking me?" I asked with a nervous twitch.

"Just hang on, this will only take a few minutes," he said, reminding me of a city cab driver.

We were flying... it felt like it anyway. I couldn't see the speedometer, but we were going over the speed limit. It was dark out and we were moving too fast to see anything out the window... just a blur.

"What's this about?" I asked. He decided he didn't hear me. He seemed a little snooty, like he was too good to be talking to a punk-ass kid like me. He had seen a million of them, I'm sure.

About thirty seconds later we sped into a parking lot... looked like a bar. The officer got out of his car, leaving me in the back seat.

"Hey!" I wailed. What gives?

I heard shouting from inside, and foul rap music flooding out as the doors were opened. *Barf.* I couldn't stand that kind of music. *It's not music!* "At least add some guitar," I told myself.

As I sat there, I wondered how my girlfriend was doing. Probably wondering where I was. Normally, I would have been home already... and she would know because she lived next door to me, well... across the street, and she knew when I left work.

My family moved into our new house about six

months ago. I was in my senior year of high school, and my parents dropped the bomb... we had to move. They didn't give much of an explanation, even after I asked. I lost all my friends... moved away from everyone and everything I knew. What a drag... I hated it.

Well, until I met Sue. What a girl. Super cute, dirty blond hair, almost as tall as me. And petite, actually... perfect. She's hot! Who am I kidding?

Gunshots made me pop back into reality. I was still cuffed behind my back and couldn't move, and I got nervous. It's not like I was able to get out and run, or even hide.

Then I saw Officer Smith dash out of the bar and run to the vehicle. He opened the door and jumped in. "Time to boogie!" he shouted. (How cheesy. I couldn't stand catchphrases. What does that even mean?)

He slammed the car into reverse, then into drive just as quickly. *Are we chasing someone?* I hadn't seen any other vehicle. Something didn't seem right... (And who was shooting the gun?)

I felt uncomfortable. *Why was the cop taking me along for his joyride?*

It was starting to get cloudy, and a little warmer, but it wasn't too bad for June. Fresh air replaced the thick, muggy fog that normally lingered. If I hadn't been arrested, it would have been the perfect night.

The squad car turned a corner, then took off like a *Formula 1* racecar, squealing its tires. "You know you can get a ticket for that?" I jested. Either he hadn't heard me, or he just wasn't amused. (Engrossed in driving?) My curiosity had spiked, but my efforts to resolve my intrigue went unnoticed. Something was amiss...

We were picking up speed... the car seemed to float on the road, like a boat going down stream.
What was happening? I could have been home by now. Why didn't he just give me a ticket and leave me alone? What a hard ass... a buzz-kill.

The officer cranked the wheel hard left. I thought we were going to end up in the ditch... but he kept it going.

"Damn, you should have driven *Formula 1* or something," I said, as I had thought earlier, trying to be funny. He didn't seem to care, and why would he?

We picked up speed again... I had no idea where we were. The trees and houses were flying by so fast, I felt dizzy looking out the window. I shook my head and took a deep breath.

I started thinking about Sue again. I hoped she wasn't worried about me... or mad. She probably thought I had extra cleaning to do at work, or was having an intense conversation with the manager, which happened often.

One time I was late, and she accused me of

being out with another girl. Typical female. Hah. Jealous because they care, right?

The sound of squealing tires broke my thoughts, and I started to fear the worst... I was momentarily weightless, then thrown against the door with a grievous jolt. My head bounced off the roof.

The car started doing misty flips and I was tossed to and fro. My face smashed the window. I could hear glass shattering, and the crunching sound of twisted metal.

I slammed the door again, hands still cuffed behind my back. End-over-end we went. Pain shot through me like a bolt of lightning... and that's when everything went black.

Two
"You like Jell-O?"
NARRATED BY SETH

"Hey sweety, can you hear me?" I recognized my mom's voice, soft and soothing, like any mother's voice should be. She sounded concerned. She sounded a way... that I wasn't used to. Then I opened my eyes.

"Hi Mom," I managed to choke out. It was kind of hard to speak, my throat was dry and scratchy. My tonsils were raisins. "Where am I?"

She looked down at me confused. "You're in the hospital dear," she said. A tear ran down her cheek. Then she grabbed my hand and started bawling her eyes out. "I'm so g-glad you're okay," she stuttered, sobbing.

"What happened Mom?"

She looked at me confused again. "Oh honey." She managed to take a deep breath, and wiped tears off her face. She sighed and looked at the floor. "You don't remember?" Then she turned to look at me solemnly.

"No..." my voice trailed off, trying to think. The TV was on, it was playing the news. Who wants to hear the news laid up in a hospital bed? Not me, typically. But I didn't care, my brain was too fuzzy to watch anything intelligent. "I don't remember anything Mom." I felt a rush go through my body... my nerves, adrenalin, fear... "What happened?" I repeated.

"Well Hun... it's kind of hard to explain. The cops are trying to piece everything together," she said, brushing her dark hair out of her eyes with her hand.

"Like what?" my voice cracked.

"You were in an accident with a police officer. You... you were in the back seat of the car. They found the minivan on the side of the road, near where you work," Mom told me. It was strange... I couldn't remember any of that! But why? "It's fine Seth, none of that matters now. Nobody even knows why you were in the back seat of the squad car," she said, shaking her head. "Hun, what's the last thing you remember?"

"Um... I remember... gee... I don't know. I remember coming home from school and playing video games, but I don't know if that was yesterday... or the day before..."

"Seth... you've been here for three days," she paused. "They put you in a medically induced coma... and pumped you full of pentobarbital," she sighed. "You're in bad shape Hun." Her eyes welled up again. Her lip quivered a little. *Mom please don't...* I couldn't stand to see her cry, especially over me. "But the doctor said you should make a full recovery. You have a broken leg, and some broken ribs. Your face is all bruised, and they think that..." she got quiet.

"Mom what's wrong?" I paused. "Mom?"

She cleared her throat. "Well sweetie, you may have suffered some brain trauma from the accident. But we're gonna take care of you Hun... no need to worry."

Was she telling the truth? Could it really be?
I wasn't sure how to feel... and I didn't know what to say.

"I love you Seth, now get some rest," Mom said. "They're going to bring you something to eat soon, so that's good." She smiled at me for the first time that night.

"Okay, I love you too," is all I could manage to say.

"Visiting hours are over Ma'am," a woman said. Must be a nurse. *I wonder if she's cute...*

"Okay then. Seth, I'll see you tomorrow sweetie! You should be out of here in a couple days. I'll bring you a Rubik's cube to play with," Mom said, giving me a wink.

"Okay Mom, ha-ha, thanks," I said waving to her. "I'll see you tomorrow."

"Bye Hun!" she said, then turned and walked around the corner, and into the hall. I sat there looking at the last place I saw her, picturing her still standing there, smiling at me.

And then I thought about Sue. Mom didn't tell me how she was... didn't even mention her. Sue was probably going ballistic over me, not knowing what happened. *Crap*... I didn't want to think of her being upset, it made me feel uneasy. *I wonder if the hospital would let me call her...*

I started gazing around the room for a distraction. Pretty dull. Sky blue walls with a few black marks and streaks along them. A border about waist high, with pink diamonds and dark green leaves in the middle of each diamond. Bizarre. There was one little light, hanging in the middle of the room. It swayed slightly when people walked under it.

There was a big window to the far side. It made the room feel more like home. At least I could see some of the grey, hazy sky. A big mirror hung on the wall too. *Creepy*. The doorway was out of sight, but I could still see who was coming in through the mirror.

Then, I saw something move out of the corner of my eye. I turned to see a man sitting in the bed next to mine, his skin was missing from his forehead... I could see his skull. The left side of his face appeared bludgeoned black and blue, and caved in. His right eye was hanging out of its socket, swinging like a pendulum when he turned his head. And I saw a piece of sheet metal, about two inches by seven, jutting out from his jugular. Blood was running down his face and neck. Then... as I stared... he opened what resembled his mouth, "Time to boogie!"

At that moment, everything that had happened three nights prior came flooding back into my cranium, exploding like a vial of Francium-223.

"Oh God no... ahh!" I gripped my face with my palms, trying to shield myself from what I had just seen.

I remembered it all... leaving work, getting pulled over by a pig, cuffed in the back seat, and... the accident.

What the hell was that cop thinking? Aren't they supposed to have special training?

His eye... just hanging there... I want to barf... Could I even look again? I knew it was the cop. No one could tell by looking at him, but he said, "Time to boogie." He even said it the same way, with this slight momentary disguise.

Still covering my face, I realized I hadn't heard Officer Smith say another word, or burp, or fart... or even breath. It was eerily quiet next to me. I took a deep breath and put my hands into my lap.

The guy must have thought I was a real asshole... looking at him, then screaming. I hope I hadn't made the guy feel worthless. And... why wasn't anyone helping him? He was on the verge of death...

I decided I should try to talk to the guy and have a normal conversation... if that was even possible. I didn't want him to feel unwelcome. I suddenly felt bad for him and wondered if he had a family. I hoped for *their* sake he didn't. If that makes any sense.

In a nonchalant manner, I gazed around the room, avoiding his direction at first. Then I turned my eyes toward the cop and stared at an empty hospital bed... *What?*

"Excuse me?" I shouted. I didn't know what else to do. I waited a minute, and nobody came. "Hello?" (You would think people in my condition would get a faster response time.) I rolled my eyes to myself. *Probably taking bets on who dies next...*

"Hello, Mr. Lynch, how are you feeling?" a nurse asked as she walked in. She sounded like she was greeting an infant. I'm surprised she didn't ask if I needed a bottle, or a blankie. *I'm losing my mind...*

"I'm fine... I guess. And you can call me Seth. I've never really liked the *Mr. Lynch* thing." *Wow, that sounded dumb...*

"That's fine sir," she responded. "How are you feeling right now?"

"I'm not in any pain, if that's what you mean, but..." I paused for a moment. "I'm sorry, but...

where did the cop go?"

"Excuse me?" she said, still smiling.

"The accident I was in... with the cop... he was right here! Did he get up and go wander around or something? I think I would have noticed if he got up... to go to the bathroom or something..." I babbled, confused.

"Hun, I really don't know what you're talking about. You've been in this room by yourself for two days," she proclaimed, staring at me.

"He was just here!" I raised my voice, then apologized. "Wow, I'm so sorry. Am I seeing things?" I asked rhetorically.

"Well, maybe," she said, with a little too much enthusiasm.

"Seriously? Do you mean that?"

"Well... you did suffer some head trauma. You have a severe concussion. It might stay with you for a while." She started shifting around, acting uncomfortable. "Things may seem out of place. You might get spouts of confusion, and-or headaches. You may even suffer hallucinations. It's rare, but sometimes that happens to people..." her voice got quiet.

I looked down. I didn't know what to say.

"You gonna be okay Seth?" the nurse asked.

"I guess so," I said, feeling drained.

"Right, good attitude! You..."

"How will I know if I'm getting better... or

worse?" I interrupted. "If I start seeing things, can I stop it? Can I control it?"

"Oh no, you shouldn't concern yourself with all that now, you need to rest," she said, walking over to fluff my pillow. She smelled nice, like freshly picked lilac. She also had the perfect smile... with teeth you can only get by having braces at some point in time.

"Thanks," I said. I liked the attention. It felt rather good. Probably the IV drip talking but, it was the best I had felt in... three days, I suppose.

"No problem, Hun." The nurse turned to leave.

"Wait! You said I've been alone in this room for two days now. So... who was in the room with me when I got here?" I wanted to see the look on her face... but she already knew why I was asking.

She turned back and said, "I'm sorry to have to inform you like this... the officer involved in your accident, he was next to you, but he passed away the first night in," she paused. "Did you know him?"

I just shook my head... speechless. He *was* next to me... I could still smell his cologne. But guess what? No one would ever believe me. *Do I believe myself?*

As the nurse began to leave, she turned around and said, "I'll have someone bring you a snack. You like Jell-O?"

Three
"My Little Sister Laura"
NARRATED BY SETH

I spit my oatmeal back into the bowl. "Yuck! What *is* this?" I asked, with a look of disgust on my face.

"What's wrong Hun? Does it taste okay?" Mom asked me.

"It's really salty," I said, dropping the spoon.

"You always love oatmeal in the morning."

"I know, but... it just doesn't taste right," I said, looking around the kitchen for something else to eat. I decided to hobble over to the cupboard to grab a Pop-tart.

The doctor said I had to be on crutches for a few weeks. It's kind of a drag. These things hurt my armpits. And I almost fall over *all* the time. But I guess I should count my blessings. I'm alive...

Leaning on one crutch and setting the other against the counter, I bent down to open the cupboard... and stared at a bunch of pots and pans. "Uh, Mom, did you rearrange stuff? Where did the food go?" I asked muddled.

"That's never been a food pantry, Hun. What are you looking for?"

"Wanted to grab a Pop-tart but..."

"Are you okay?" she asked concerned. "They are over here, to the right," she pointed.

I slowly backed myself up and opened the lower cupboard. To my astonishment, I saw the Pop-tarts... along with other snack items.

A chill ran down my back. *What's going on?* I wasn't about to accuse Mom of lying, I'm sure she wasn't. Did she rearrange things and forget? My head started to throb and pulse like one giant neck vein.

I sat down and opened the foil. No need to toast, I liked them just the way they were. I began to munch. The flaky pastry filled with who-knows what, didn't taste very good either, but I dealt with it. I wasn't going to *starve* myself.

Dad was at work. He's kind of short, but strong. He likes to work out at the gym. He has short, dark hair that's thinning in the front. You can't tell by looking at him, but he's very intelligent. He's a repair man for some gas and electric company. I don't understand it all, but he likes it. Sometimes I think Dad has a money tree in the backyard, he always has a lot of cash on him.

And he adores Mom. She is always smiling, especially when he's home. She's about an inch shorter than he is, and petite, with dark, shoulder-length hair. She worked as a cashier for a long time, but Dad let her quit when he landed the job he has now.

But you know, she's the sweetest mother in the world, always so kind and optimistic. She often says, *Time fades the stains of life.* At least it sounds positive to me, but I'm not sure.

So, Dad lets her stay home and be a housewife, and she loves the idea. It works out good for everyone. The bills get paid, and the house always looks and smells nice.

"Just think, you'll have plenty of time to practice your guitar now that school's out... and you still have weeks off from work, at least before they expect you back," Mom said, trying to motivate me, trying to distract me... not from her, or anyone else... but myself.

"I guess you're right. That's a good idea," I said, picturing the guitar she bought me about a year ago. It was fun, but I could already tell, it would take determination to become good at it.

Summer vacation wasn't starting off so well for me, but I was hoping things would get better. I had about three months before college started. Enough time to hang out with Sue, go see movies, and party. Thirteenth grade was my parents' idea anyway, and I couldn't find a good reason to argue with them. Then, I *should* be able to find a better job, rather than working at *The Burger Barn* for the rest of my life.

My two friends from school Ed and Jeff come over often... we play video games or go places in Ed's boxy, '89 Chevy Caprice. Ed plays the drums, though he's not very good at it... but he tries. Sometimes we get together and jam in his garage. (Now all we need is a bass player, and a singer who doesn't make the neighbor's dog start to howl.)

I'd hang out and play with my sister Arielle sometimes too. She's seventeen, one year younger than me, but we are *nothing* alike. We both like to play sports, but all her other interests make me think she's from another planet. She likes hip-hop and sometimes listens to boy bands. That being said... I listen to loud, thrashy music. Grunge, hardcore, heavy metal... you get the idea.

Arielle is pretty, with transparent red hair, and brilliant blue eyes. She has the most beautiful face. And how? The rest of the family has dark brown hair, and brown eyes. My face looks like a frying pan. I was never immensely popular with the ladies.

But Arielle, she's smart, and very outgoing. In just a couple months at our new school, she became one of the most popular girls. All the other girls wanted to be like her, and all the boys just *wanted* her. Straight A's and everything. I'd probably think she was stuck-up... if I didn't already know better.

All the guys at school were wasting their time anyway. She seemed to have a crush on the guy next door, Jason. I think he's my age. He was in my class, for the short time I went to North Lake High.

He's originally from Boston... and still has a little bit of an accent. He seems cool... if he doesn't cross my sister. He doesn't want to find out how protective I can be. I'll snap his neck in a second... or at least try.

But they both giggle when they are around each other. I catch him staring at her like he's never seen a woman before. Kind of creepy.

"You want some scrambled eggs? I made too much," Mom said, stuffing her face.

"I'm good. That Pop-tart was just enough, but thanks Mom," I said, holding my gut to show emphasis.

I stood up and walked over to the trash can and tossed in the partially crumpled up wrapper. "You know what... I *will* have some eggs." *Why not...*

Anyway, as I was saying...

My little Sister Laura is super adorable. She's nine and a little firecracker, so full of energy, jumping off the furniture, dive-bombing Spunky, our Fox Terrier. Nobody seems to notice... and she never hurts him, or herself. She's like a cat that always lands on its feet. She has dark, curly brown hair and big, brown eyes, like I said. And a cute, little button nose.

She's quiet though, doesn't say too much. Lately, when I talk to her, she just smiles. When I ask her a question, she just shakes her cute, little head. It's okay if she's quiet. It doesn't bother me.

Laura really loves her dolls... she has a big collection of them. She's always carrying one around, swinging it in her arms. It's like her security blanket or something.

I think Laura gets her love for dolls from our grandmother. She must live with us now since she became too old and fragile to look after herself. Grandpa died when I was just a little boy. I don't even remember what he looked like. But Grandma chugged along despite her sadness.

She was always baking home-made apple pies, especially in the summer. In wintertime, her house always smelled of roasted meat. Maybe turkey, or beef, but it was a nice aroma. It gave the feeling of being home, her house was just so cozy.

Grandma's getting old now. Her hair is all white. She has shrunk like a new cotton T-shirt in hot water. Lately though, she's been a little ornery, always mumbling words under her breath. Now I think she's just waiting to die.

"I'm going outside to work on the garden, do you need anything before I go?"

"Nah, I'm okay Mom," I said with a smile. I took another bite of scrambled eggs, then crutched myself over to the living room to watch TV.

Flipping through the channels, I found nothing interesting on. Then Laura came in and jumped on the couch.

"Hi Seth, what's on?" she asked, bouncing up and down on the cushion, her curly hair bouncing with her.

"Not much, why... you want to watch cartoons?" I asked. She smiled and nodded her head. So, I handed her the remote, then leaned my head against my arm and shut my eyes. I must have passed out...

* * *

When I opened my eyes, I saw a dark, dingy ceiling. I was lying on a hard surface that felt like wood... splinters were poking me in the back. I looked to the side, the wood was green and black colored... kind of moist and rotten looking.

I was in some room, not noticeably big. There seemed to be an array of strange looking tools on the walls.

Then I noticed the smell... sulfur? I wanted to gag. I went to plug my nose but couldn't move my arms.

I realized I was chained to the bed, or wooden platform. Both of my arms and legs were bound with ropes, and I was naked. I tried to shake free, but there was no use. *What is going on?*

The heat... why is it so hot in here? I could feel beads of sweat rolling off my body. I had a hard time breathing in the thick, decaying air... worse than any summer day I had ever experienced.

Everything glowed red... the lightbulb dangling in the middle of the room was colored.

Where am I?

Turning my head, I noticed someone standing in the corner, facing away, wearing black... just standing there.

"Hello?" I watched, waiting for something to happen. I was scared... my whole body shaking. "Who are you? Can you help me?" I waited for a response. "Why am I here?" Still nothing. "Hello, can you hear me?" My voice became dry and raspy... I started to cough.

The figure in black turned around. I gasped at the sight. It looked like a woman, but with the face of... she didn't have a face... just an amorphous blob with a mouth, and a slithery tongue sticking out, all slimy and gross looking.

It started to move... walking gangly toward me. It opened its mouth revealing rows of sharp, yellow teeth. Drool fell in puddles from its lips. Nasty snarls of black hair hung from its skull in all directions. The thing snapped at me as it crept closer, grinding its teeth. Slimy, tendril-like veins bulged out all over its skin.

I tried to free myself again but found it impossible. The more I moved, the more the ropes burned my wrists.

"Help!" I shouted as the grotesque creature made a cacophony of sounds. It crept even closer, its joints seemed to pop in and out of place as it walked. Then it stopped and smelled the air with its forked tongue, somehow... looking hungry. *Please don't eat me... I don't want to be dinner... I probably don't taste very good...*

My whole body started to tremble violently. More beads of sweat hit the ground.

The creature took a few more steps, then stopped next to me. *It's all over... I'm dead...*

Its slimy tongue slithered out, and it growled, "The doctor will be with you... soon."

What?

The creature bent down and sank its teeth into my abdomen, then yanked out a mouthful of my flesh, veins dripped with blood, tissue flopped out onto the wood.

I screamed in agony... seemed pointless, but it dulled the pain. The creature reached down for seconds and gobbled up the remnants. My intestine and perhaps my pancreas hung out of its mouth as it masticated. My screams echoed off the walls...

* * *

"Ahh," I woke up, still sitting on the couch. I had perspired all over myself. My shirt was drenched and stuck to me. For a second, I thought I had died and gone to hell. (I'm not a fan of bad dreams... but who is?)

Cartoons were still playing on the TV, but Laura was gone.

I decided to try to get ahold of Sue again. I needed a distraction, plus I hadn't seen her since the accident. Now that I think about it, she hadn't tried to get ahold of me this entire time... how many days has it been?

I picked up the phone and dialed her home number. My hands were still shaking, I had to dial twice to get it right. After a few rings, someone picked up.

"Hello?"

"Is Sue there?" I asked. It was her mom. "Okay," I said, being placed on hold. I waited for a moment.

"Hello?" Sue answered.

"Hi babe, how have you been?" I asked.

"Good, I guess," she said with disdain. I noticed immediately she wasn't acting like herself. She's usually all bubbly.

"What's wrong?" I asked, sensing something amiss in her voice.

Silence...

Then I added, "I came over the other day and your mom said you were out with a friend. Then I called the next day, and you weren't home then either. Did you even come to see me in the hospital? What's up? I haven't heard from you all week..." I shut up and waited for a response.

"Seth, I think we need to talk," she said after a pause. *Here we go...*

"Okay... about what?" I asked.

"I did come to see you, and... you weren't responsive. I was so scared."

"Okay... and?" I asked. She was beating around the bush... it was too obvious.

"Well, Seth... I moved on. I didn't know if you would ever come out of it. You seemed like a vegetable."

"W- what...?" I fumbled with my mouth.

"I'm with someone else now," she added.

"At least give me a chance! I was only in the hospital for a few days! What the hell is wrong with you?" I could feel the blood rush to my head. But then I knew... her plan was to leave me all along... a subconscious seed sown in opportunity... I never stood a chance.

"I'm sorry Seth. I still care about you... maybe in the future we'll be together, and..."

"Who's the other guy?" I asked, trying not to choke up.

"You don't know him," she said plainly.

"I knew it, there is someone else!" I yelled. Then silence...

"I already said that..." she muttered. Then more awkward silence. "Okay, I gotta go Seth," she finally said.

I was trying to fight the tears, but they came anyway.

"O... k-kay" I choked out. I swallowed hard and regained my composure. "Do you still want to hang out? Be friends?"

"That's probably not a good idea Seth," she responded quickly. *Why does everyone hate me...* "I'm sorry," she repeated.

"Yeah-yeah... see ya," I said and slammed the receiver down as hard as I could. There was nothing left to say. *What the hell...*

* * *

That night, I went to bed thinking about my graduation party my parents were letting me have. Nothing big really, Ed and Jeff were going to stop by, probably play some games, hang out, and drink a few beers.

Arielle Invited a couple of her friends over just to bug me, and the neighbor kid Jason. Him and I don't click. I'm not sure why, but I just don't seem interested in trying to be his friend. Calling him an acquaintance is appropriate, and I think he feels the same way. It's obvious we just tolerate each other.

Mom and Dad were sketchy at first about us having beer, but I reminded them that the legal drinking age *used* to be eighteen when they were young. They looked at each other dumbfounded. Then Dad said, "We'll be chaperoning... I mean it, nobody's getting crazy, understood?" Of course, I agreed with him.

I hoped they would be chill, and not embarrass me this time. Dad thinks it's funny to tell jokes, the same ones he heard when *he* was a teen. Nobody wants to hear that...

I laid on my back in bed, trying to pass out. My body was tired, but my mind was awake. I started talking to myself in my head... *I think I want banana peppers on the pizza tomorrow... yeah, and onions, extra sauce, and all that other yumminess...*

What about a movie? We have a thousand of them. Or should we just listen to some music? I have an awesome stereo system. One time, my neighbor came pounding on the door, claiming he couldn't hear his own TV over my stereo. Anyway... it rattles the windows. For the price, it's very...

-Thwonk-

"What the hell was that?" escaped my mouth. Something above me hit the floor, interrupting my thoughts. The sound made me jump through my skin.

The only thing above my room is the attic... Nobody is allowed up there, at least not us kids. Mom and Dad said to never go up there. They said it's off limits, just because it's old and dusty, the floorboards are weak, and there's nothing to see anyway... they say.

In the whole six-plus months we have lived here, I don't recall ever going up to the attic. I wasn't that fascinated by old floorboards much, but was still curious... what made that noise?

I would have normally gone to investigate, but being in a cast, with crutches for legs, made me feel defeated in that moment. My chest still ached, and I really didn't feel like getting up. *Probably just a pile of old boxes that finally fell over...* "Yeah, that must be it."

But then, I thought I heard footsteps above me. Very soft and still. I held my breath and tried to focus.

Nothing... just silence. I must be hearing things again, I thought morbidly. *I must be hearing things...*

The full moon created an array of silhouettes on my wall. They all danced when the wind blew. It happened every time. I continued to watch the shadows frolic across the way. Even with my eyes closed, they were still dancing. Minutes ticked by, but eventually, I fell asleep.

Four

"The Teddy Bear"
NARRATED BY SETH

I hobbled over to the kitchen table and sat down for another *delicious* bowl of oatmeal. I mixed the strawberries & cream flavor with the blueberry and was praying it would taste better today.

"How was getting down those stairs this morning?" Dad asked with a smirk. He thinks I'm crazy for wanting to sleep in my own bed upstairs when the couch is on the *first* floor. But I'm stubborn. I'd rather combat the stairs for a few minutes, than sleep on that intolerable couch. My back feels broken when I wake up on that thing.

"It's getting easier, I just push through it."

"Good man," Dad said, sipping his coffee.

Arielle walked into the kitchen. She was trying to eradicate a monster eye booger. Then I noticed she was wearing one of my Nirvana T-shirts.

"Yo... why are you wearing my stuff?" I asked aggravated. She just turned to me and stuck out her tongue.

She grabbed a glass from the cupboard and opened the fridge for the milk. Then she made a B-line for the peanut butter, (she likes it on toast in the morning). "Don't stretch it out!" I lectured, swallowing another bite of oatmeal.

"How does that taste this morning?" Dad asked.

"It's fine today," I lied.

"Good, good. I was getting nervous for a minute there," he said quietly.

"Nervous about what?" I asked, questioning the look on his face.

"Well..." he hesitated. "Didn't the nurse explain it to you?"

"A little, but..." I shrugged my shoulders.

"Oh... well, like the doctor said, a concussion, or slight brain damage could cause your taste buds to be off like that," he sipped some coffee. "But so can a cold, so... I guess if you're getting better, I'm not to worry."

Thanks for being brutally honest Dad...

I smiled, kind of fake though... obligatory. I knew my dad... he didn't seem as convincing as usual. So naturally my reaction was that of despair, at least in my mind.

Occasionally, the countenance on someone's face is forced by circumstance, and there is nothing they can do to extinguish it. But Dad hadn't seen my face... he was too busy reading the neighbors Sunday newspaper.

"So that's good, that means you'll be able to taste the pizza later," he laughed and sipped more coffee. "By the way, I need to order that soon... you guys want wings too? Soda? I have to make a trip to the store so just let me know."

"Oh, I forgot. I heard a real loud thud from the attic last night... I mean, it sounded like something fell to the floor," I explained, watching Arielle's eyes get wide.

"I'm sure it was nothing," Dad said. "But if you would like, I can go check it out..."

"Don't worry about it, probably nothing," I said. "Maybe some old boxes finally fell over. "I couldn't think of anything else to say.

At that moment, my head began to throb. As in a vise, it felt like it might split in half. I felt dizzy and the room began to gyrate. I cried out in angst and clapped my hands over my face.

"Are you okay?" Mom asked me in haste.

I couldn't answer her right away, nausea was creeping in. *What is happening to me?* I sat completely still, holding my temples. *Please God, just make this stop...*

I sat there for a few more seconds, until my head stopped pounding so hard. I finally looked up and scanned the room. Everything was fuzzy and cloudy. Then someone spoke, but I couldn't understand their words. "Htes... era uoy yako?" *Was that Mom?* Her voice sounded low, like in slow-motion. "Yeh... htes!"

"Wha..." I choked out. *What is she saying?*

"Are you okay?" Mom repeated nervously.

After a few moments, I managed to speak. "Eh... I guess so," I said weakly. I stared at the wall, confused. My head still throbbed but was relenting. My heart rate returned to normal. After a few moments, things started to seem real again. "I guess I'm just tired is all," I said. Mom looked at me and sort of cocked her head sideways. She knew I was being insincere.

Then I watched Laura stroll into the kitchen, holding a stuffed Teddy bear. Spunky, who was sprawled out next to the wall, let out a deep growl as Laure walked by. She was holding the bear tight, squeezing the stuffing out of it, then sat it down in a chair like it was a person. "Look who showed up in my room!" She pointed to the Teddy bear, with this animated smile on her face.

Arielle turned around and saw the bear and dropped her glass of milk on the linoleum. It hit the floor with a clanging *pop*. "I'm so sorry, I'll clean it up!" she said frantically, grabbing paper towels and a broom. Dad just shook his head, then walked over to the bear.

"Hey, check this out! It's an original *Morris Mitchum* Teddy bear, named after former President Theodore Roosevelt," Dad stated. He's proud of his trivial knowledge. "These old bears are made with animal fur and stuffed with thin wood shavings."

"That's cool," I said, watching Arielle clean her mess.

"Where did this come from?" Dad asked.

"Laura brought it down," I said, trying to stomach another bite of oatmeal.

"Who did?" Dad asked, looking confused. Then I watched him step on a piece of glass. "Son of a... really?" he cried, hopping on one foot. Blood started dripping to the floor.

"Oh gosh Dad, I'm so sorry," Arielle said, sweeping the bloody piece of glass into the dustpan. She looked around, "I think that's all of it."

"Good," Dad uttered with aggravation. "Now I need a bandage," he said, walking out of the kitchen.

It's strange... I saw the look on Arielle's face before she dropped the milk, just briefly. It was almost like the stuffed bear had scared her. But that doesn't make any sense... she's a tough girl, what's there to be afraid of?

* * *

We started the party around noon, and the few guests we invited trickled in a few minutes later. Arielle was showing off, trying to be cool in front of her kind-of-new friends. They were all doing girly stuff, so I didn't pay much attention to them.

(Mom said it was only fair that Arielle got to invite a few friends too... anyway, it kept her from bugging me. Plus, one of her friends was cute.)

The guys and I set up a table from the garage and played a few rounds of beer pong. It was Ed and I vs. Jeff and Jason. I was sinking them like Shaq. No – no – no... Michael Jordon. (MJ is way better, Shaq just shoves people around.) It was fun, I always win. So, I didn't end up drinking that much... probably better off that way.

After rocking out to the Deftones and eating pizza, we went to chill in the basement and play some pool. My parents were lucky enough to find a house with a big, finished basement, so we got to keep our billiards table and air hockey table when we moved. It's fantastic.

Playing pool was a little awkward with a cast on my leg, but I could still stand good on one foot. I missed a few easy shots...

After crushing Arielle and her friend Stacy at air hockey, Mom called down to us to start cleaning up. We all helped pick up the trash and put leftovers away. I was the last one to reach the top of the stairs.

"Hey man, that was fun. You know, when your leg heals, we should start that hacky-sack tournament you were talking about," Ed said enthusiastically.

"Yeah dude, I almost forgot!" I'm a hack wiz. *No*

one can stop me! We once had twenty-two people in a kill-hack circle, and I won six times in a row. The only reason I lost the seventh game... I started boasting and talking crap. *What's wrong... did you forget how to play?* The last three guys teamed up against me. Live and learn... *to keep my big mouth shut...*

That's when the lights went out, the music stopped, and it got eerily quiet inside.

"We're all gonna die!" Ed hollered. A few people chuckled.

"Nah, I think maybe we tripped a breaker," I said. I was in the electric trade program my last two years of high school... I learned a few tricks.

Dad came stomping down the hall. "You guys good?"

"Yeah, no problem," I said weakly.

"Okay. I'm going down to check the circuit panel," he said, looking slightly irritated.

"Yeah, that's what I was thinking too," I said, watching my dad walk around the corner. "Ed, let's gather these trash bags and go out back... try out that new dragon pipe you got," I said with a cheese-grin.

"No doubt son... no doubt!" he responded in a goofy voice.

We were scrambling to put the last beer cans in a garbage bag when I heard a long, painful shriek come from the basement.

"Dad!" I shouted, after recognizing his voice. I couldn't exactly run to the basement door, but I watched Ed trot over through the darkened room.

He leaned into the cellar doorway. "Mr. Lynch? Sir, are you okay?" he asked, walking down the steps. I grabbed up a crutch and followed.

Arielle came running around the corner. As I looked at her, I tripped over something on the floor and fell. Swinging my arms didn't help in the least... and I ate the edge of the coffee table.

-Crack-

"Son of a..." I wailed as I hit the floor. I sat there still for a moment, then touched my mouth and studied my hand. Blood ran down my fingers. The sight made me queasy.

Arielle stared wide-eyed. "You just sounded like Dad," she uttered, laughing. Then she leaned in. "Damn, you lacerated your mouth pretty good!" she added, getting a closer glimpse of my face.

"Thanks a lot... want to help me up?" I asked, still on the floor, wiping blood off my mouth with my T-shirt. I looked to see what I stumbled over but saw nothing. "What the heck did I trip over... air?" I asked, kind of aggravated. Arielle grabbed me by the arm and helped me to my feet. "Thanks," I mocked, kind of rolling my eyes.

The lights came back on, and the LED display on my stereo started buzzing around. The digital clock my mom keeps in the kitchen was flashing

12:00. *Dad must have reset the breaker...*

Arielle decided to go venture downstairs to see what was going on. I heard some talking but couldn't make out what was being said. Then I heard footsteps on the stairs. Ed came back into view. He turned and waited for my dad to climb back up.

When Dad finally reached the top, he turned to look at me. "Feels like I got *stabbed!*" he announced with a little fright in his eyes. There was blood on his hand. "I don't know what happened. I was feeling along the wall... grabbed a flashlight to see what I was doing, then walked over to the panel. I had only been standing there for a few seconds when I felt this horrible pain in my side. I don't know if I *backed up* into something sharp, or what... but wow!"

Backed up into something?

Blood was pooling through his shirt. It was a lot more than what was trickling from my mouth. I heard my sister finally walking back upstairs.

"Arielle, would you drive me to the hospital?"

"Sure Dad," she said, grabbing for her purse. "You know, if you lose too much blood, I could donate a quart to ya," she chuckled. "Sorry, just trying to lighten the mood."

"That wouldn't work," Dad said with a strange look in his eyes.

"What do you mean?" Arielle asked, kind of

shocked by his answer.

Dad didn't respond to her question. "Can we get going? I'm in a lot of pain," he barked.

Arielle turned and gave me a look of confusion, then waved bye.

I watched Dad step outside with a grunt. Arielle followed close behind and then shut the door.

Mom was at the store again. She had forgotten a few things like always. Everyone had gone home by now, except for Ed. My little sister Laura was around somewhere, probably playing patty-cake with her dolls in her room.

"Well, that was freaking weird, huh?" Ed chimed. He started biting his bottom lip.

"I guess *so*," I paused for a moment. "I need to change and put ice on my face." I picked up a crutch and began the journey to my bedroom. "This will only take a minute man, just hang out for a few," I told Ed, lifting my good leg to the first step. After a few minutes I managed to get to the top.

In my room, I tossed my blood-stained T-shirt into my hamper. Then I grabbed the first shirt I saw off the floor and put it on.

My room's walls were plastered with band posters, mostly because I liked them, but they also helped cover up the awful, yellow wallpaper.

I needed to clean too, I realized. Clothes and junk covered most of the floor. I hadn't organized anything in quite a while. Dust bunnies crowded the corners... occasionally they would get up and dance. But there was too much on my mind to care about cleaning.

I stumbled my way back down the stairs and to the kitchen. Walked through to the freezer to get a bag of frozen peas. I also grabbed a washcloth to wrap the peas in. I could feel my face swelling from hitting the coffee table. The cold peas would help a little. Walking, on the other hand, had become even more difficult.

"Let's go out back behind the barn," I told Ed, fumbling the peas. Ed picked up the vegetables for me and we made our way out the side door. It was perfect outside, hot... but without the piercing death rays from the sun. The clouds gave most of the backyard some shade.

"Mm... nicotine..." Ed said, lighting a cigarette. He started shaking his head frantically and making noises like Beavis does. He's such a character... never a dull moment with this guy.

We got behind the barn where I have a couple chairs and a patio table set up. Ed proceeded to pull out a little baggie and the pipe shaped like a dragon. "I brought Scooby-snacks!" he said, waving the bag in the air.

"Nice," I said, trying to keep my balance. "I would have brought out a hack, but..." I stopped. We both knew I couldn't play hack in this cast, but the thought of it was amusing.

Ed handed me the loaded bowl, and I sparked it up. "This is supposed to be Maui Wowie," he said all stoner-like. I swear, he's just like Jim Breuer from the movie *Half Baked*.

As I exhaled, Ed said, "Setsat doog thgir?" My head started to feel funny, and my right ear started ringing. I set the pipe down, closed my eyes, and held myself up against the small patio table. Everything was spinning, dreamy. Then I heard in the distance, like through a thick fog, "Uoy t'nod kool os doog nam."

Feeling sick, I opened my eyes and slowly glanced up. I saw Ed take a drag of his cigarette, and that's when his face began to melt...

His cheeks drooped. One eye seemed to sink below the other. Then pieces of his flesh peeled off his skull and flopped to the ground.

Worms started crawling out of his twisted nostrils, and his sagging ears. He took another drag from his cigarette, and puss started oozing from his eye sockets. As he exhaled, a cockroach wriggled out of his mouth...

All I could do was scream...

Five

"Bullseye"
NARRATED BY SEAN LYNCH

I gassed up the riding lawnmower, getting ready to sweat in the midday heat. There was a nice breeze that balanced out the sun's scorching rays.

After a few minutes of mowing, I noticed a twinge in my side by my kidney. I'm still not sure what happened yesterday. It was a clean, deep cut that needed a few stitches. Though mowing was the cause of my sudden pain, probably from the vibration, it was a nice diversion. *A catch twenty-two...*

I felt my skin burn as I focused on all the stuff in my yard. There were a few trees to mow around, and the kid's old swing set that nobody played on... at least the barn in back against the woods took up some space... half filled with junk from the previous owners. *Go ahead, just leave all your crap for the next guy.* I rolled my eyes at the thought.

I looked over at Bob's yard, my neighbor.

Freakin' Bob Fletcher, what a tool. He has a nice car though... I'll give him that much. It's a Camaro, probably a '96 or '97. (I'd rather have one that's ten years older to be honest.) A dark grey color, very *low pro* looking. He parked it facing my house, at the end of his driveway. *Put it right in my face why don't ya!* It's just like him to show off... but it's a nice car. Maybe I'll get one someday. Black... most likely black.

Past the Camaro, Bob had some targets set up in his backyard. I've seen him out there a few times arching. He has a nice compound bow and arrows with little frills on the ends. I was never good with a bow. Bob seems to like it, and he's a good shot...

Spunky ran right in front of the mower, chasing after a bird flying low between the trees. We've had him now for about five years. He will attack just about any other creature that crosses his path. For such a little guy, he is fearless. And the kids adore him.

The kids... Seth. Poor guy. It kills me to see him suffer the way he is. The other day I called the doctor, telling him I thought Seth's condition was getting worse. But he told me not to worry. "Don't pay any attention to his hallucinations," he said. Why? Wouldn't that just make things worse for him... and convince him his delusions are real? *Seems like child abuse to me. I don't understand...* But then again, I never went to medical school.

A loud *clunk* made me jump. Then a cracking sound invaded my ears. I felt blood rush to my face. Beads of sweat formed on my scalp. I knew exactly what had just happened... but was afraid to look. *Just because I'm paranoid, doesn't mean he's not after me...*

I spun my John Deere around and noticed a big crack in Bob's Camaro windshield. I had run over a large stone, sailing it through the air. *A nice spider-web where the catcher's mitt should have been...*

"What the hell..." I choked out. My mouth got dry... my palms got even more sweaty. (Bob isn't exactly the guy you invite over for tea and crumpets. He's a prick... there's no other way to put it. He will curse at anyone who looks at him cross-eyed.)

Bob must have heard the *clunk* and *crack* too... he was already outside walking toward his car. *It's only a matter of seconds... then he'll see it...*

I didn't want to, but my better judgment told me I should man-up to my mistake. There was no need to escalate the situation any further. I shut down the mower and jumped off.

"Hey ass-wipe... you do this to my car?" Bob called over to me. I waited to get closer to answer... I didn't feel like shouting.

I approach him with a humble-mannered gait, not puffing out my chest like I might normally do. I wasn't necessarily afraid of Bob, but more afraid of the damage he could inflict...

"I must have run over a stone with the mower," I said waving my arms around, trying to influence him with my own agitation.

"Well nice shot Einstein," Bob belched, putting his hands on his hips.

"I know, I'm really sorry about that, I'll..."

"You're gonna pay for that window!" Bob rudely interrupted.

"Yeah, I was planning on it... can't you just..."

"What the hell were you thinking man?!" Bob wailed, thrusting his fists around.

"I was thinking... first of all, let me get a word in edge wise, and then..."

-Whack-

Bob blasted me in the jaw. I instantly saw stars. Pain shot through my face and down the rest of my body. I hadn't noticed, but I must have fallen over into the grass. I gazed up into the sky and grabbed my palpitated face with my hand, trying to make the pain subside. I could taste blood now.

"That's for running your mouth," Bob decreed, like the pompous ass he was.

Slowly picking myself up, I walked up to Bob and stared into his eyes. This evil grin spread across his fat cheeks. He looked satisfied that he had knocked me on my ass. *I'm going to wipe that smirk right off your ugly face...*

And that's exactly what I did. I swung at him as hard as I could, contacted the center of his grill, and turned his nose into Old Faithful. Blood squished out and splattered on the lenses of his glasses. He staggered back, making a gurgling sound, like he was drowning in his own blood.

He grabbed his face. "*Ugh*," he cried out in pain. "You'll be sorry... *hack*... you'll be sorry you did that, Lynch," Bob said with defeat in his teary eyes. He stumbled backward a few more steps. "If I wasn't choking on my own blood... *hack-hack*," he coughed and spit. "You'd be a dead man!" Bob turned and hustled up to his front door and vanished inside.

"That's enough excitement for one day," I told myself. I didn't finish the yard... I was too angry to care. My body was shaking, and my face was throbbing. Maybe tomorrow...

Six
"In the Dark"
NARRATED BY SETH

I choked so hard I nearly threw up. Trying to pass the pipe to Ed was taxing, my arm was convulsing from coughing. "Whoa killer," he said jokingly.

We continued to walk downtown, past the police station, restaurants, and commons. Then we crossed main street to get to the pier.

Jeff was supposed to meet up with us. He lived nearby. We hadn't seen him yet but were keeping an eye out for him.

It was a peaceful area. The houses along the pier were built bungalow style, like on stilts. They seemed to all float on top of the water, especially in the dim streetlights.

The sky had grown dark, and we were trying to enjoy a burn-walk before curfew. Nobody else was around. There were a few houses to the right, and nothing but water to the left. You could hear some seagulls perched on rocks nearby, probably fighting over leftover French fries from the nearby

McDonald's.

"I'm sorry about the other day man," I sighed. "I didn't mean to scream in your face like that."

"Bahahaha, man... you had me *tweaking*. I thought you were going crazy, for real," Ed proclaimed like a hippie.

"Me too," I confessed. "I don't... damnit... I don't know if I can trust reality... it's like..." I didn't finish my sentence. I couldn't find the words to explain how I felt. He probably didn't want to listen to me ramble on about *my* problems... everyone had their own.

"I wonder where Jeff is," Ed said. I could tell he was trying to change the subject. But not for selfish reasons... not because he wanted to shut me up... I think he was trying to help me forget about my condition. "He should have been here by now."

"My parents act like nothing is happening to me," I refocused on myself. "I told them what happened the other day, about how your face melted off, and..." I was trying not to choke up. "They didn't even care! They shook their heads and carried on with their day. They just accept it now, that I'm losing my *mind*... I guess," I trailed off, thinking how insane I must seem to Ed... to everyone. *I need help...*

That's when I saw someone in the distance. "That must be jeff," I said, turning my head.

But Ed was gone... I did a double take, then

spun around in a circle. He was nowhere to be found. "Ed," I yelled, squinting in the darkness. "Where'd you go?" *How could he disappear that fast without me noticing? How? There's nowhere to hide...*

I stood in the middle of the street, looking dumfounded, watching the person in the distance continue to approach.

I kept walking toward the loop-around. The pier had parking spots along the way. A few cars were parked close to the houses, but as I got closer to the loop, there were no cars. Not much of a scenery at night anyway. Sometimes when there's a full moon, I like to come out here and watch the glistening moonlight on the lake water. Seems so surreal. It's a good place to bring a hot girl on a date... when you're broke.

Not like tonight. There was no moonlight, and fog was sailing on top of the water. I did, however, discover the sound of waves splashing against the rocks to be comforting.

The mysterious, dark figure turned and walked toward one of the floating houses. *Okay... so that's not Jeff... where is everyone?*

I decided to turn around and head back to my house. *Those guys must be playing a game with me, trying to scare me or something...* "Ed," I shouted one more time and listened. I looked around... glanced behind me. Nothing but the sound of waves.

The lake was to my right now, and I could see a boat docked in the distance. The docks were cement, looking aged and weathered. They had steps that went down to the loading area, near the water level. After a heavy rain, you couldn't step down in without getting your shoes soaking wet.

I continued walking, kicking stones as I went. All alone in the dark, I just stared straight ahead, watching cars go by in the distance.

Then I saw something start bulging out of the water by the docks ahead of me. It looked like a bald head emerging... creeping up slowly. Then a neck and shoulders... a torso. *What the hell is that thing?*

I kept staring as the figure climbed the stairs of the dock. Water dripped off the creature's gaunt body. It walked as if trying to be still but had uncontrollable tics that forced it to move.

The creature reached the top of the stairs, turned its head, and looked right at me. Its eyes were black and huge. *It looks like a Grey... an alien...*

Its skinny, naked body and scrawny arms and legs glimmered from the streetlights. Its head was unproportionate from its body. I saw a small line of a mouth, and two holes where a nose should have been. I didn't see any ears... but that didn't stop it from hearing me.

I took a step back and my sneaker scraped over loose stones in the road. That made the creature leap at me and growl. My knees began to buckle. I stumbled backward but caught my balance. The Grey continued to approach me... like a dog inching toward its prey. *Why did it growl at me?*

It seemed to float off the ground as it walked. The alien came closer, and with an outstretched arm, it reached as if to strangle me. Through telepathy perhaps? *Death by Tele-Stomp... forward, down, low kick. That was Quan Chi...*

I didn't want to stick around. I went to run but felt glued to the pavement. I couldn't move. *I can't move...*

The alien started making clicks and choking sounds with its wrinkly lips. The noises came out slow and goopy. Then once again, I heard a dog barking in the background. The creature clicked some more, then cocked its head sideways... staring.

I went to speak, but only a squeak came out.

Nothing makes sense. Is that Spunky barking?

The Grey opened its ugly mouth wide, and it stretched, and contorted, until it enveloped me. Its mouth seemed to stretch out into eternity. Blackness filled the space all around me. *I hear a dog barking again...*

I felt as if being sucked into a black hole. I tried to hold my position but couldn't feel the ground. I began to fall... the sensation was real... I was falling helplessly into darkness.

* * *

Suddenly, I landed hard on my back. A whoosh of air escaped my lungs as I hit. That's when I opened my eyes and stared at the ceiling. I sat up in bed, drenched in my own sweat. I looked around dazed, then rubbed my eyes, trying to focus through the dim light. "I hate this," I whispered to myself.

I flipped my pillow over and put my head down. Then to my astonishment, I heard the alien growl again... *huh?!*

My body immediately tensed. I got chills all over and covered my face with my comforter. *Is that monster in my room? There's no way... no way!*

I held my breath and listened... then feeling like an idiot, realized... it was my *dog* barking and growling. I could hear the little guy outback. My chest was still thudding audibly. I took a deep breath to calm down. *What is he freaking out about?*

There was more growling. Some more barks... this time farther away. Then a squeal. "Maybe I should go check on him."

That's when I heard Spunky let out a horrible, death howl. He bellowed like he had been attacked by a wild, ferocious animal. It was a kind of screech I had never heard before.

"Oh damn," I uttered, jumping out of bed. As

swiftly as I could, I put on a pair of cargo pants and a T-shirt, picked up a crutch that was lying near my bed, and hobbled out of the room.

I walked softly... I didn't want to wake anyone. *Did anyone else hear Spunky outside?* Either way, I needed to find out what was going on. *Maybe I should wake someone, they would be quicker than me...*

The stairs were a nightmare. Trying to take them one at a time, and be stealthy without falling on my face, was quite a task. I finally made it outside without causing a problem. The barking and growling from Spunky had ceased. *I hope the little guy is okay...*

I had heard him getting farther away, toward Bob's house. *Prick.* I figured I might as well search my yard first for any clues, it would take a minute either way.

Dad always kept a flashlight in his trunk. *You never know when you'll need it*, he'd say. So, I limped over to his car and popped open the trunk. *Wow, what a mess. It's going to take me two days to find it...*

I started shuffling through junk. Old rags with motor oil on them, soda cans everywhere, a busted-up blue tarp shoved in the corner, a stack of ripped magazines, and... a flashlight, yes! I grabbed the light, shut the trunk as quietly as I could, and started for the backyard.

The sky was eerie looking. Moonlight trickled through the cirrus clouds that covered most of the sky. I passed the bushes by the driveway and continued to my backyard. I could see some of Laura's toys lying around. She never picks up after herself, but that's typical for a nine-year old.

I continued shining the light through the grass, but to no avail. The yard was quiet now. No sight or notion of Spunky, not even the crickets were making a sound...

I shined my light into his doggie house, but it was empty. I started to investigate the woods nearby but saw only shadows of foliage. I kept walking along the brambles, hoping to spot him.

The feeling of being watched was all around me like a fog. Not necessarily *someone*... but I felt something evil nearby, watching... stalking me from the bushes. *It's out here... I can feel its eyes on me...*

I looked up in the distance, over to Bob's yard, trying to shake the strange feeling. *What's his last name again?* Oh well, I didn't care. Dad didn't seem to like the guy very much either.

The flashlight beamed through his backyard, and I prayed nobody was watching. I looked past an old swing set, past a stack of firewood left over from winter, then noticed something moving fast... away from the woods toward Bob's side yard.

What the heck was that thing? From a distance

it looked like a cub running upright. But that's not possible, is it? *Must have been a big racoon or something... maybe...*

At this point, I didn't care if Bob saw me, I needed to find my dog. His yelping was my first concern. Realizing he wasn't in my yard made me anxious. *He was on a chain...*

"Spunky," I called in a whisper. Still nothing. The only sound was the breeze and my sandals in the grass, which made my feet cold and wet from the dew.

I resumed my walk back by the woods, where Bob keeps his archery targets, (you know, those big ones that are four-foot tall, with rings of different colors). Anyway...

As I approached the first target, I got a bad feeling. My lungs felt tight. Something was wrong. I took a few more steps. *What is that, hanging on the target?* My jaw dropped when my eyes focused.

Spunky appeared to be standing on his hind legs, leaning against the target... but with an arrow sticking straight out of his chest... an array of blood splatter was behind him...

I must have screamed loudly, because the next thing I knew, the neighbors were outside. "What the hell is going on out here?" Bob demanded, bursting outside, his wife standing behind him wearing a nightgown.

I saw our porch light turn on, and Dad rushed

out the back door. He let the screen slam shut behind him.

"What's all the commotion about?" Dad yelled angrily from the porch.

I threw my hands in the air with dishevelment. I turned my gaze back to Bob. "What did you do?" I asked, pointing, trying to hide my emotions.

"What the hell!" Bob shouted in surprise, taking notice for the first time. "You ruined my target... you got blood all over it... and what the hell is that thing?" pointing to the deceased canine.

"That's my dog asshole... how could you?" My eyes were tearing up, seeing him stiff like that, his head down... defeated.

"I didn't do nothing... why would I? And ruin my own equipment?" Bob asked smugly. "Those things cost hundreds of dollars!"

"Well, I sure as hell didn't shoot my own dog!" I lashed out.

"My bows are locked up kid. I didn't do it..." Bob said calmly, a little remorse in his voice.

I sat there for a moment, confused. Dad had walked up next to me. He heard the whole conversation. I guess neither of us knew what to say. At first, I thought Dad was going to attack Bob. Dad had a devilish look in his eyes. But it seemed like Bob was telling the truth, and Dad saw it too. I'm sure he didn't want another fight on his hands, so he just shook his head.

"Sorry about your target Bob," Dad said bereaved. "I'll help clean it up or... buy you a new one, whatever it takes."

"How could this have happened?" I asked, shivering from the night cold, I suspect. I wiped tears from my eyes. Nobody said a word...

Dad walked over to Spunky's lifeless body. He snapped the arrow right in half like a twig and pulled the white-haired dog off the arrow shaft. Bob just stared at us the whole time.

We walked home quietly. Dad held Spunky in his arms. then looked down at him. "I'm sorry boy," Dad sniffled. "I'm so sorry..."

We dug a grave for Spunky at the far end of our yard by the woods. It was the middle of the night, but it had to be done. Dad wiped sweat from his forehead, then laid the lifeless dog in the hole... you know the rest...

Seven

"The Secret"
NARRATED BY ARIELLE

I poured a bowl of Cap'n Crunch berries, (it's my favorite). Then I grabbed a spoon and the jug of milk from the fridge and sat down. I started dwelling on the day... what to do. *Maybe go to the mall... go see a movie...*

I wondered if Jason would go with me. He's so cute, but he doesn't know I think that way... yet. He looks like Tom Cruise, or a slightly chubbier version of him... and that's okay with me. Who wants a scrawny guy anyway?

I took a bite and felt milk dribble down my chin. I quickly grabbed a napkin. Mom was making her normal Sunday breakfast, but I don't really care for any of it. She makes blueberry pancakes, bacon, eggs, and toast. Sometimes she even fries up some hash browns. Yuck! They can eat all that garbage... I don't want it. I'll eat a pancake occasionally, but I must be in the mood.

"Have you seen the paring knife?" Mom asked,

turning toward me. "I haven't seen it in a day or two."

"Umm, not sure Mom. I haven't used it lately," I responded. She continued to flip her bacon strips, then grabbed a knife of superfluous size. Silverware always seems to disappear. We are down to four spoons... how does that happen? *I guess underwear gnomes need to eat too...*

Anyway, Sunday is usually the only morning Grandma will come down for breakfast. She loves blueberry pancakes. She always smothered them in butter and maple syrup. It felt odd she had not yet graced our presence this morning.

Ugh... you know what? I've been having thoughts. They put me in a dark place. Are they strange thoughts? I don't think so. Like... why am I the only redhead in the family? That can't be normal. That's *not* normal. I think anyone with a brain would come to the same conclusion, based on observation alone.

So many thoughts swirled in my head. The way they treated me... sometimes I felt like I was just a visitor, and not part of the family. I can't really explain it. I tried talking to my friend Beth about it, but now she thinks I'm crazy. Not, *stay away from me* crazy, but more like, *roll your eyes* crazy.

I look nothing like Mom... or Dad for that matter. It's not like it was yesterday that I started to notice. Maybe I should just stop driving myself crazy with this... but it's stuck in my mind like a parasite, it just won't leave. Sometimes, I picture bashing my head off the wall. Should I be concerned?

"Where's Grandma?" Dad asked, smiling at me. "She's usually on her third pancake by now," he said, walking around the corner. I assumed he was going to check on her and make her come downstairs for some breakfast.

"Where's Seth?" I asked, putting my empty bowl in the sink.

"Dad said he had a pretty rough night," Mom reported.

"How so?" I asked.

"Umm... you notice anything missing this morning?" Mom asked with a sad look in her eyes. I looked at her with a puzzled expression. "Seth found Spunky dead last night..." Mom said slowly.

"What..." I choked. "What happened?" I asked, trying not to cry.

"Maybe we shouldn't talk about it right now," Mom said.

I became troubled. I started thinking... maybe it was *my* fault that Spunky was dead.

I'm such an idiot...

You see, I have a little secret... and no... I'm not telling you. But I think I messed up. I messed up big-time... and I don't know if I can ever make it right again. Maybe there is a way... maybe I can reverse it... but nothing would bring Spunky back. That, I could not fix.

Dad came running down the stairs, tripping at the bottom and nearly falling face first into the wall boarder. "She's gone..." he said out of breath.

"Where would she go?" I asked, taking another bite of cereal.

"No. She's not breathing," he sighed. "Grandma's dead," he explained with sadness in his eyes.

"What!" Mom turned around in a panic, and swiped the pan of scrambled eggs, sending it swiftly to the floor. The pan crashed hard, and eggs went flying everywhere. "Mom... Mom!" she wailed, running up the stairs.

I ran after her to Grandma's room. When I looked in, Grandma was sitting in her rocking chair. Her eyes were wide open... a look of fright plastered on her face.

No, not again... Please, just let it be a heart attack...

"Oh, dear God..." Mom gasped, seeing an object hanging out of Grandma's mouth. It resembled a doily. Mom slowly pulled the doily from her mouth... wiping tears off her cheeks with her other hand. When the object was removed all the way, I could see it wasn't a doily, but one of Grandma's dolls garments. A little frilly, white dress, made for a super short, tiny, porcelain girl.

"Mom, how come I don't look anything like you? or Grandma?"

Mom started freaking out. "Seriously?! That again?! This is not the time Arielle..." she said indignantly. I put my head down. I knew it was bad timing, I just wanted a reaction...

Mom redirected her attention to the dead woman in the chair. "What's going on?" she agonized. "Why was this in her mouth?" She turned around and looked at me like I had the answer. I just looked wide-eyed at her. *Poor Mom. I haven't seen her this upset since... I think ever...*

Mom began yelling and stomped out of the room. I instantly felt my face get hot. My pulse started to race. My palms perspired. Somehow, I knew it was all my fault... *didn't I just get done saying that? What is happening around here? My head feels funny... déjà vu?*

For some reason, life didn't seem so authentic anymore. I wanted to rip my hair out and start screaming.

Spunky and Grandma were lifeless... within twenty-four hours of each other.

I must fix this...

Intermission
"Chunky"
NARRATED BY ADAM
(Spring 2017)

"Last call of the day and..."

-Barf-

"Aww... you nasty!" Tanya exclaims. Matt had interrupted my story. He puked right in the circle, right next to my feet. I think some splashed onto my shoe.

"Gross," Desiree says looking away.

I need a smoke...

"You good Matt?" I ask.

"Yup," he smiles, taking another swig of his beer.

"That's insane. If I get sick, I'm done. See you in the morning," Tanya says laughing.

"Now we have to move the fire or... start a new one. I'm not looking at that all night," Eric says, his face disgusted, his speech slurred.

"Why is it chunky?" I hear Desiree whisper to Eric. They both laugh.

"Alright, let's move the seats, move the cooler. I'll grab some more wood." I'm kind of annoyed that I have to grab more logs, but I'm a pyromaniac. Setting things on fire is amusing...

We all huddle in a new circle, around a pile of twigs and a couple bigger logs. The chilly, night air is settling, I try to keep my legs moving to prevent shivering.

Desiree moves her chair over to the circle. Eric hasn't moved yet. I begin spraying lighter fluid all over the twigs. That's when Eric falls over, right off his seat.

"You drunk bastard," I shout. He throws his arm in the air and gives me a thumbs-up.

"Aww, look at Eric," Tanya says laughing.

"Damnit Eric, why?" I scoff, slightly amused. I walk over and grab Eric's arms and drag him through the grass to the new circle. Then I let his arms slap the ground.

For some reason, he reminded me of an escapade we had, probably a year ago. Eric and I and my girlfriend at the time went to the bluffs. We decided it would be cool to grab a 12-pack and walk along the lake's rocky cliffs... some around twenty feet tall. *How did we get the beer? We were all underage... I can't remember...*

Anyway... we walked for probably thirty minutes looking for a spot to finally relax and crack open a beer... but it didn't happen as planned. On top of the cliffs were woods... dark, thick, and mysterious. It was becoming dusk, and the tide was coming in like a bull after his matador. We had no choice but to scale the rocks.

We took our time, being cautious. I was trying to balance myself while walking on the treacherous stones, carrying beer at the same time. You can't drop the beer.

We eventually came to a resting spot, but we were trapped! It was like being king of the hill... in checkmate. To the left was water, straight ahead and to the right were walls too high to climb. We couldn't even backtrack without breaking our legs.

I started to get nervous and looked up at the sky. By now, it was dark, and the waves were crashing against the shore, making loud, thunderous collisions with the rocks.

To my surprise, above me, I saw the reflection of fire bouncing around in the tree leaves. I cupped my hands around my mouth, tilted my head back, and shouted, *Is anyone up there?*

A few seconds later a guy came over to the edge. He shouted back to his friends, *There are people down here!*

Grab a long stick and help us up! I said, losing my fear. The guy came back with a long tree branch and hoisted us all up to the top of the cliffs. One by one, we made it to solid ground.

There were two guys and two girls in their

group, huddled around a small campfire. We introduced ourselves and explained how we ended up in such a predicament. Not one of my brightest ideas... but we all had a laugh about it afterward.

"How much longer is the story?" Tanya asks.

"Um, I'm almost halfway," I respond.

"So cool, I can't wait!" she says with a cheese-grin.

"Yeah, the second half... it gets kind of brutal." I pull out a cigarette and light it, then bend down to ignite the twigs. The fire roars up high. "Let there be light!" I say, raising my arms in the air. Tanya laughs. "Anyone else want a beer?" I ask quickly.

"Shoot," Desiree chirps. I grab two out of the cooler and toss one to her.

I crack mine open and take a swig. Then head over to the woods to take a leak. "Be right back," I say. "I have to piss."

"Me too," Matt blurts out.

I walk up to the woods to relieve myself. I watch my shadow shrink against the trees as I approach. Matt walks off in the other direction.

"What am I supposed to do?" Desiree asks.

"I don't know, find a place to squat," I respond laughing. I take another drag then flick the cigarette in the woods. *What a refreshing night... so peaceful...*

Reaching to zip up, I hear some rustling in the bushes... right next to me. It's too dark to see anything inside the trees, so I take a step forward and listen.

Nothing.

But then I see two glowing eyes. A fiery red glow, just hovering. Then they disappear... more rustling sounds.

What is that?

I squint my eyes to get a better look. Then the glowing red eyes appear right in front of me. Startled, I cry out and step back.

A creature leaps out of the woods screaming, its red eyes pouncing. I yelp like a little girl and fall backward onto the grass, the monster falling right on top of me...

Its mouth opens wide... fangs covered in drool... and reaches down to take a bite. "No... Please," I beg softly, struggling to push the creature off me. Then a hand reaches up... and pulls off the mask.

"Gotcha dumbass!" Sara shouts.

I was so relieved knowing the hideous creature was only a mask. She got my blood pumping.

Sara stands up and continues to laugh at me. She lives next door... we hang out almost every day. Her main goal in life is to scare the hell out of me... all the time! "You're too easy," she teases.

"Nice one," I retort, feeling embarrassed. "I spilled my beer! And I think I pissed on myself a little." She laughs at that too... such a sweet girl. "You wanna hang?" I ask. "I'm telling the story. I have a new audience... you know... besides Eric," I laugh. "He's probably passed out now anyway."

"Yeah, I'll hang for a while, sounds cool," she says. "And happy birthday!" she adds, skipping over to the fire.

I can't believe I've been driving for two years already... it doesn't seem like it. And now I can legally buy my own smokes...

I introduce Sara to Matt, Tanya, and Desiree. They all say hi and are overly friendly.

"How far along are you in the story?" Sara asks curiously.

"You're about to find out," I smile, sipping my beer. Then I reclaim my place and continue...

Eight

"Easy Money"
NARRATED BY SEAN LYNCH
(Summer 1998)

Last call of the day and then I'm going home, I told myself. I lit a smoke and changed the radio station. It was kind of cloudy outside. Fog had settled heavy all around. It was hard to see two cars ahead of me. Overhead signs were impossible to read, and the streetlights were faint and dingy.

-Honk-

I blasted my horn as a guy pulled right out in front of me. I had to jack the brakes and cut the wheel ever so slightly. Some tools went flying off the seat, spilling onto the floor. Damn, I can't stand bad drivers. *Get off the road!* Then it occurred to me... he probably couldn't see my lights either.

I continued eastbound, taking a well needed drag to calm my nerves. I finally found my way to Pleasant Street. Some young woman was pushing a stroller down the sidewalk, probably headed for the park. The road was full of potholes. Chunks of pavement were hanging out by the curb. What a dump, I thought. *Pleasant street...*

I had to find a big, old, dark-green house, set back from the road. Some elderly woman lived there. She called and complained her furnace wouldn't shut off. *It's the beginning of summer, why is she even messing around with it?*

I dodged a few more craters in the road, then spotted the house through the trees. I pulled in the drive and made my way through the dangling branches to the poop-green colored house. *At least her driveway is smooth...* I came to a rest and turned the truck off.

I grabbed a few tools from the passenger side floor and proceeded to the front stoop. I gave the door a couple of raps and waited. The door swung open and a short, wrinkly, old lady with nappy, white hair stepped out.

"Thank heavens," she said with a raspy voice. "I didn't know what to do. My furnace has been running for hours and it won't stop. Thank you so much for helping me."

"No problem, ma'am, it's my job," I said trying not to sound rude. The old lady seemed a bit slow, but sweet, nonetheless.

I stepped in and asked where I might locate the furnace. She had boxes piled high along the walls, and a raggedy throw-rug in the middle of the living room. The lady gestured for me to follow her down the hallway.

"It's right around the corner," she said, taking short steps. Her legs shimmied as she walked. "I was trying to take the filter out to vacuum it, and it just turned on. It startled me to death," she said, pointing to the filter.

"I see. Well, let me run a diagnostic and see what her problem is." I grabbed my little pocket flashlight to get a better look. This was an older style furnace, but I've worked with all kinds.

Right away, I noticed a little knob. It read: *Push Man./Pull Auto*. She must have bumped into it when attempting to free the filter, I realized. All I had to do was pull the button out for the *Auto* function, then the thermostat would see it's too warm and shut off. "Well ma'am, give me some time and I'll have her fixed right up for you," I said with a smile.

"Oh, thank you so much kind sir." She really was a sweet, old lady. "Would you like some water? Or some tea? I make a good cup of black Jasmine!"

"Thank you, ma'am, but I'll pass for now," I said. The thought of drinking that tea made me shudder. I like sweet, iced tea though, that's good stuff. "Just trying to locate the problem," I told her. Of course, I already knew what the problem was...

I started taking out screws and disconnecting wire nuts... making it look good... killing time. I grabbed my multimeter and was testing voltage...

for no reason.

After twenty minutes, I went out to the truck and grabbed a few old parts that I didn't need. I strolled back inside and continued to boondoggle.

I put everything back together, and pulled out the button, setting the furnace back to *Auto*. All done. *I've killed enough time here...*

"Ma'am, it looks like your thermocouple went bad, and the hot surface igniter was just about to snap in half, so I replaced that too. But all in all, I think it's in good shape. It shouldn't come back on until the fall when you will need the heat," I explained.

"Thank you so much kind sir," she repeated warmly.

"It's all in a day's work," I said. Pretty cliché I know, but I must play the part.

I walked out to my truck and wrote up her bill and shoved my tools back where they belonged.

Easy money. I could do this all day...

I hopped out of my truck and jogged up to the woman, rocking in a chair on her porch. "Here you go ma'am. I hope you have a lovely day," I said and turned to leave.

"$674? Oh my... why is this so much?" she asked humbly, her eyes going narrow.

I quickly turned back to her. "Well... your furnace is incredibly old, so the parts are rare, kind of hard to find these days. Sorry Ma'am, it's just how business works. You have a good day now." I turned and walked down her driveway.

I got back into my truck and headed home. It was about a twenty-five-minute drive. My AC was busted, but I probably wouldn't use it if it worked... I preferred to have the windows down...

The drive seemed to take longer than usual, but I got to see a huge family of deer along the way, (I almost hit Bambi). Then I cranked the classic rock station. "Take the Money and Run" came on and I began to tap my fingers on the steering wheel. The song was ending as I pulled into my driveway. Such a good tune, I thought.

I was home a little early. I assumed the kids were hanging out with friends somewhere. Seth hobbling around somewhere on one foot... Arielle probably out shopping like always...

Allison was home, probably doing laundry, or cleaning the kitchen... or enjoying her crafts that she was into.

I stepped out of the truck and walked down the drive to check the mail. Nothing but junk... and the electric bill. Not overly exciting. I turned back and walked up to the front portico.

I was surprised to see Allison and Seth in the foyer as I stepped inside.

"Hey babe," my wife said. "You're home early."

"Yeah, I ah... I got tired. I didn't have any more house calls, and I sure didn't want to go hang out at the shop, so..." I trailed off. "What are you two doing?"

"Seth here had another episode. He insists on going to see the doctor."

"For real?" I asked.

I gave her a look. She knows the look. The way I positioned my brow down, and the slight one-sided smirk, was saying the doctors might not be a good idea. We were already told to ride it out. Doctor Hunt even told us it's best to try to ignore Seth's cry for help. *It almost sounds like child abuse...* but Doctor Hunt seemed to think Seth would get better, if there was less attention drawn to his condition.

But how are we supposed to do that? I can't help but feel his pain and wish for his immediate amelioration. I hate to see my children suffer, but he seems to be improving and that's all I can ask for...

"Well, I'm in a hurry, I want to beat the traffic," Allison said, dropping her car keys on the tile floor. She bent down to pick them up. "Oh yeah, I picked our birthdays for the mega lotto today. 2- 6- 58 and 12- 1- 61. Why not, you never know," she added, shrugging her shoulders.

"I'll cross my fingers, ha-ha," I said, smiling. She stepped toward me and gave me a kiss goodbye.

"We'll be back whenever, see you later Hun," she exclaimed. They stepped outside and headed to the car.

"Bye babe, see ya Seth. Everything will work out, okay?" I shouted from the porch. They turned and waved. Then I went inside and shut the door. I prayed the doctor would have some idea on what to do, anything that would help my boy.

I walked into the kitchen. I figured I would fix myself some food before I showered this funk off me. I grabbed everything needed to make a sandwich. *I'm sure Allison isn't cooking dinner now. Fend-for-myself day...*

I piled some roast beef and cheese on a slice of honey wheat bread.

Then I heard a *thud* from upstairs. I didn't think anyone else was home. *Maybe Arielle is here after all...*

I finished making my sandwich. I grabbed a handful of salt and vinegar chips to go with it, (so good).

I sat down on the couch and inhaled the roast beef. I turned on the TV and watched an episode of *Seinfeld* while I ate my early dinner. I cracked open a refreshing Mountain Dew to wash it down. I laughed at the TV, *you got to love Kramer...*

When I was finished, I walked into the kitchen and put my plate on the counter, then went upstairs to shower.

I climbed the stairs like a slug, I was beat. I didn't really have any reason to feel exhausted, but sometimes your body just wants to rest.

I walked past the bathroom and noticed the shower was already on. *Hmm... must be Arielle.* I then proceeded to my room. *Might as well at least change my clothes... on second thought, I'll grab clothes and go to the downstairs bathroom.* I rifled through some T-shirts and grabbed a pair of sweats.

As I walked out of my room, approaching the bathroom, I heard soft whispers and giggles. First my daughter's voice... then a man's voice...

There's a random dude in the shower with my seventeen-year-old daughter...

A rage fumed up in me like never before. Ever felt like killing someone? This was the time... (look up *pissed-off* in Webster's, and you will see *my* face).

I was now *The Incredible Hulk*... and before I blinked, I was already in the bathroom, I had already opened the curtain, I had already grabbed the guy by his throat... and was holding him by his neck, six inches off the floor against the wall. The wall fractured and gave way as I slammed him against it.

The shower was still running, splashing on my arm. Water dripped off the boy as I held him there... though, I wasn't the only one holding him against his will... his newest antagonist was fear.

My adrenaline had spiked so much that I had no

problem holding the kid up, choking him. His lips were turning blue, and he started to make gurgling sounds. Then he scratched and pawed at my arms...

"Daddy... don't kill him!" Arielle screamed. "Please let him go!" She turned the water off. Eerie silence filled the room, besides the *drip-drip* of the faucet, and the gasping of air from my victim.

I started shaking. *How dare you violate my daughter! You son of a bitch...*

"Daddy... please!" Arielle shouted again.

After a moment, I released my grip, and let the kid fall to the floor. He grabbed for his throat and forced air back into his lungs. "Pick up your clothes and get out of here as fast as you can," I said, gnashing my teeth.

I backed up to give the kid some space. He picked up his pants by the legs, then his shirts and socks. He hadn't noticed his wallet had fallen from his pocket... onto the floor against the sink cabinet.

He bolted from the bathroom carrying his belongings. Then I turned to Arielle. "What were you thinking?" I asked her, trying to calm down, trying to be sensitive, but I was still shaky. I was pissed! You have no idea. But yelling never solved a problem around here. A soft voice in rebuke seems to be more effective. So that's what I did.

She looked up at me, towel wrapped around her. "I'm sorry Dad," she said. Of course, that's what she would say. What else *could* she say? *"He loves me and I'm pregnant and we're getting married,"* would have been harder to swallow.

"We'll talk about this later when your mother returns," I blurted out. "For now, go hang in your room... alone."

She accepted my plea and went to her room.

My heart was still pounding. I punched a hole in the drywall. White dust shot out from the gap. My knuckles started to ache.

Damn, what a day. I could use less of them if they keep ending this way... you know?

I wanted to kill that kid. He's lucky Arielle was still in the room... the situation may have ended differently otherwise...

I glanced down and saw the kid's wallet leaning against the cabinet. I bent down to pick it up and looked inside. "Jason..." I thought I recognized the neighbor boy. Great. How am I supposed to resolve this one? If I say anything to the kid's dad, he'll probably want to fight again. *Macho man...*

I glanced at my skinned knuckles and the new modification I made to the wall. *So, what am I supposed to do about this? Hmm...*

Before I closed the kid's wallet, I took out a $20 bill and shoved it into my pocket.

Nine

"Bear Claw"
NARRATED BY SETH

I came out of the bathroom and headed toward the stairs. As I stepped down, I saw Spunky come into view. He went straight to the front door and stared at it. *Someone needs to go outside...*

I trudged my way downstairs and grabbed his leash hanging on the wall. He started jumping up and down all excited. It happens every time.

Outside, he immediately wanted to chase the birds bathing in the front lawn. Apparently, it had just rained a lot, there were little pools of water all over the backyard. But the sun was out, glistening over the puddles, creating a mirage of blinding, white glint.

Spunky sniffed around, getting his nose all wet. Then he sneezed, his whole body convulsed. "Gosh buddy, you good?" I asked rhetorically. He came over and nudged his face on my leg, so I bent down to pet him. "Good boy," I said, the way anyone would typically speak to an animal.

Through the opened kitchen window, I could hear the phone ring. I quickly took Spunky off his leash and hooked him up to the dog trolley. Running on the deck I nearly biffed it but caught my balance. I finally got to the phone and picked it up. "Hello?"

"Dude come down," It was Ed. "Jason and Jeff are here."

"Jason?"

"Yeah, Jeff brought his bass. He said he was talking to his older brother... said he wanted to start a band and needed equipment. So, his brother lent us a bunch of stuff man, it's awesome! He brought over his old PA and microphones and cables. Even a stomp box!"

"Nice!" I said, feeling excited. "Jason?"

"Dude, grab your guitar and amp and get over here!" Ed demanded.

"Sure... I'll ahh, I'll be down in a few," I stuttered.

Why was Jason over there? I thought Ed hated him. Not hate... a strong disregard? Sure, that's it. I've never cared for the guy either, he seems like a creeper.

I gathered all my gear up and packed my car. The drive to Ed's was only about four minutes, Sometimes I just walk to his house, (but not with all this equipment).

When I pulled in Ed's driveway, the guys met

me to help carry stuff into the garage. It took a few minutes to set up.

"So, Jason, I didn't expect to see you here," I spoke up.

"Yeah, I ran into Jeff. We started talking and... this band idea came up. I try to sing occasionally so I figured... I might as well give it a shot," Jason said, placing his mic into the stand.

I plugged my guitar into the amp, turned it on, and smashed the strings. It sounded like a dying cat, so I pulled out my tuner.

Ed started banging on his drum kit, coming up with some cool beats. Then Jeff came in with a punky bass line. I finally got my guitar tuned right and joined in. We improvised for a good twenty minutes, just jamming. It sounded cool.

I started to play a solo, to the best of my ability anyway, when Jason dropped the mic. It bounced hard on the ground and started to feedback. I stopped playing and killed the volume to my guitar. Jason started to walk out of the garage...

"Where are you going?" I shouted, then walked over to the PA to stop the awful squealing.

Jason turned his head, "I have to go for now," he explained, then continued to walk down the driveway with some kind of determination, but with his arms straight at his sides. We all stood there watching...

"But you just got here man!" I yelled. Ed and I

gazed at each other with confusion. We didn't know Jason very well, but this was odd behavior for anyone...

Jason went into the street and looked down. He bent over and pull up on a manhole cover.

"What is he doing?" Jeff asked, playing his bass with the volume down.

"I'm not sure," I responded.

In awe, we watched Jason lift off the heavy, steel cover. He dropped it to the side, letting it slap the ground.

Then he jumped down into the hole...

"Jason!" I wailed. "What the hell is he doing?" I asked the other guys in shock.

We all set our gear down and ran into the street. I was the first to get to the hole in the ground. Nothing but darkness down there.

"Jason... can you hear me? Are you okay?" My voice echoed back to me. I didn't care for the guy, but I still didn't want to see him hurt. "Jason," I shouted one more time. After he didn't respond, I decided to go in after him.

"Dude, don't go down there," Ed pleaded.

"I want to know what he's doing. I know he's weird but... who does that?" I asked. "And maybe he's hurt... I could help."

I stepped into the manhole and started to walk down the rebar ladder. I got about four steps down when my foot slipped, and I fell...

My body slammed the ground, foot-ass-first, and my ears started ringing. *Damn that hurt...*

I shook my head and regained my composure, then I climbed to my feet and looked around. "Guys," I yelled up. "It's too dark... I can't see anything... Ed, do you have a flashlight?" *How is Jason walking around down here?*

"Well, yeah I think we do," he said, coughing up some phlegm. "I'll be right back bro."

"Pretty strange kid," Jeff yelled down to me from the street, referring to Jason.

"Guess so," I agreed. My voice echoed again, this time coming from behind me.

After a few moments, Ed came running back over with a flashlight. "Here dude, catch." He dropped the light down to me. I caught it and turned it on, beaming the light all around. It was damp and dingy everywhere.

"Looks like the sewer follows the road, it goes east and west," I explained. "I don't see Jason anywhere," I paused, looked around some more. "I'm going to see if I can find him..."

"Want me to come with?" Jeff asked.

"Nah... I won't be long. I'm just going around the corner. If I can't find him after like five minutes, he's on his own."

I started to head down the ass-smelling sewer, splashing nasty water all over my shoes. I held the light up in front of me. Nothing but sewer walls, covered in moss and feces. "Jason..." I called. "Hello?" I kept walking, listening for a response. I didn't get one...

It looked like the sewer curved up ahead. I came to the bend and turned the corner. The sewer opened right up into a much bigger tunnel. And beyond that, I could see where the tunnel fractured off into many different passages. Tall pillars of concrete were all around. "Jason..." I wailed one more time. I stood still and listened...

That's when I heard splashing, like someone running through the mucky water. I ran to my right, following the sound... but then it stopped. The smell seemed to get worse as time passed, almost unbearable now. I continued forward, glancing at the cracks in the ancient brick work.

"I'm down here..." I heard a voice bounce off the walls... very faint, almost a whisper.

"Jason, is that you?" *Of course it is... who else would it be?*

"I'm down here," I heard again, this time clear. It seemed to come from all directions though...

"Stop playing games man... come out already, this is getting old," I said with a little irritation in my voice. *Aren't we a little too old to be playing hide and seek? Maybe not, but there's more to this than playing games, it would seem...*

"Jason!" I yelled again, this time quick and sharp. My words reverberated off the walls, giving them a stereo effect.

I decided to pick a tunnel at random. If he wasn't there, I was going to give up. I ducked my head and started down a tunnel. "This guy is so damn strange," I whispered to myself. "We should be practicing, not walking around in this crap hole," I continued to mumble.

The tunnel seemed to get darker the further I went along. "Why would he come down here?" I asked myself. I realized hearing my own voice was the only thing keeping me sane now. The walls were even more dingy than when I entered, and they seemed to be closing in on me. *I really don't belong down here...*

I noticed more garbage lying around. Then I saw something scurry off in my peripheral vision. I shined my light on it... a big fat rat, sniffing around. I scuffed my feet and scared it away.

I kept walking, about to give up, when I came to another fork in the tunnel. I shined my flashlight down the left side, then the right. I saw nothing but darkness. *I'm done... time to go...*

"I'm down here..."

I jumped. *A whisper... where did that come from? It didn't sound like Jason that time...*

I pointed my light in the tunnels again. In the far distance I could see a figure, standing in the hall on the right side. I started walking toward it. "Jason, stop playing man... you're creeping me out." I kept walking. The dark figure didn't move, and I was fairly sure he hadn't been standing there the first time I looked...

As I approached, I recognized Jason's T-shirt. But... something was wrong. I started to regret following him down into the sewer. His shirt was all wet and torn... and covered in sludge. Tattered cotton hung off him like strips of bacon. His arms and legs looked like they had been feasted on by rats... with bloody scratches all over. An eerie presence filled the air around me. It seemed like Jason had just woken up from a dirt nap. "Hey!" I shouted again, loud and stern.

Jason turned around fast. "I'm down here," he cried. His face was bloody, his wet hair matted to his skull. He was missing teeth, and his left eye was black and blue, almost swollen shut. The rest of his skin was pale, almost green looking, and sagging off his bones. His face had fresh bite marks where you could see flesh was torn away. My stomach lurched at the sight.

He reached out his pruned, waterlogged hands. Stretched them out, like a zombie. "I'm down here, Seth. I'm down here..."

"What? No... you're... you can't..." I stopped talking and started to run in the other direction. Whoever, or *whatever* that was... it wasn't Jason anymore. It was something else. *A creature from beyond... does that make any sense? How much time had passed... maybe ten minutes? How do I explain this?*

I could hear zombie Jason still yelling for help. I didn't care. I was gone! I didn't look back. I tried to force the thoughts from my mind... his torn flesh, a weak and shaky voice that wasn't his...

It took me a minute to remember which way I had come. Eventually, the tunnel to escape came into view. I turned and ran down the hall, splashing crap-water all over myself. Winded, I finally reached the rebar ladder.

I looked up and saw nothing but bright, white light. I wondered if Ed and Jeff were waiting. Step by step I climbed the ladder to the street above. I hoisted myself up out of the manhole. It was so bright I could hardly open my eyes, (after being in that dark dungeon). My eyes started to adjust, and my heart skipped a beat. I wasn't outside. I wasn't in the street where I should have been...

"What are *you* doing out here young man?" a woman called. I spun around and saw a pretty nurse, all in white. "You're supposed to be resting in bed."

"How did I get *here?*" I asked dumbfounded.

"Excuse me sir, you need to get back to your room," the nurse said sternly.

"No... I don't belong here!"

"You were in a bad accident. You need to get back to your room, now sir!" she said persistently.

"I don't belong here... I left this place *days* ago... none of this is..."

"Sir, you're under hospital supervision now, you must return to your bed," the nurse argued, twirling a strand of hair with her fingers.

"Fat chance," I said, and took off running. *There is no way I'm going to lie down in another stiff hospital bed!* I ran around the corner and took off sprinting.

I could hear patients' groans seeping out into the hallway. An elderly man sat hunched over in a wheelchair. A woman comforting a crying baby.

How did I get here?

I looked behind me and saw a security guard chasing after me. I kept running. My wet sneakers made squishy noises as they slapped the floor.

I ducked around another corner and spotted an exit sign at the end of the hallway. I ran past a bathroom, freshly cleaned with bleach. Ran past posters on the wall, about how to perform CPR. More rooms with sick or dying people inside. Still running. I was almost there... Just a few more steps...

I busted through the door... and saw Jason. He was standing there in his tattered wardrobe. Maggots were crawling all over his face. Then he slowly opened his bloody, saggy, half-eaten mouth. "Why won't you help me?"

* * *

I opened my crusty eyes. I was in my bed. I sat up, and saw him, standing there menacingly. Water dripped off his rotten, moldy looking clothes. Maggots were still crawling on his face... all distorted and chunky... scourged, and bloody.

"Go away!" I screamed... so hard my throat started to burn. I began to shake all over and couldn't stop myself. I turned and smashed my face on the pillow. *Am I doomed to a life confined by these horrible images? Is my mind locked in a prison of its own dreadful nonconformity? I must do something... I can't take another day of this...*

When I looked up, Jason was gone. *Of course...*

The crutch felt cold on my arm as I hobbled downstairs in my boxers and T-shirt. Mom was cleaning the dishes. I walked around the corner into the kitchen. "Mom," I said rubbing my eyes. "I can't take this anymore!" I grumbled, breathing heavily. "I keep seeing Jason, dead... his face..."

"Calm down Seth, gee," she said, drying her hands off on a towel.

"I think I had a nightmare... but it seemed too real to be a dream. Me and the guys were jamming in Ed's garage, and ..."

"It was just a dream. You don't need to freak out," Mom assured me.

"No... when I woke up, he was still in my room," I paused for a second. "Mom, can you please take me to the doctor's office," I asked impatiently. I started pacing back and forth anxiously.

"I don't think you need to see..."

"Please!" I interrupted. "Take me!" I just couldn't handle it anymore. I hated yelling at Mom, but she wasn't listening to me! *It seems lately, anytime I tell her there's a problem, she just ignores me...*

She wasn't like that in the beginning. The last few days... my parents act like I'm fine... just peachy. But I'm *not* fine.

"Okay... we can go. Just... please make yourself presentable," Mom said reluctantly.

I felt a rush of relief and began to make my way back to my room. I reached the top of the stairs and decided to clean up a bit first. I went into the bathroom and turned on the hot water, grabbed my toothbrush and toothpaste and cleansed the morning funk out of my mouth.

I washed my face and looked at myself in the mirror. I noticed in the reflection, the wallpaper was peeling and cracked. The light seemed to be extra dull and off yellow. Above the peeling wallpaper was blood... dripping down in the form of words. It said, *Help Me.*

I stared into the mirror, frozen with fear. My brain was trying to comprehend what it was seeing. Then a dark shadow began to manifest behind me. My heart skipped a beat. What *is that?*

I spun around. Everything was in place. Nothing

out of the ordinary. No blood dripping. No cracks in the wall. No black figure. Then I spun back to the mirror, and everything was normal.

Come on Seth... snap out of it already.

I went to my room to get dressed. I threw on some old skater shorts and a T-shirt that said, "Rock Will Never Die." Grabbed my wallet and headed back downstairs.

"You ready to go?" Mom asked.

"Sure am," I said sarcastically. Of course, I wanted to get help, but nobody likes going to the hospital...

As I was putting on my shoes, the front door opened.

"Hey babe," Mom said. "You're home early."

"Yeah, I ah... I got tired," Dad said. "And I didn't have any more house calls. I sure didn't want to go hang out at the shop, so..." he trailed off. "What are you two doing?"

"Seth here had another episode. He insists on going to see the doctor," Mom told him, giving him a strange look.

"For real?" Dad asked. They glanced at each other some more.

"Well, I'm in a hurry, I want to beat the traffic," Mom said, dropping her car keys on the tile floor. She bent down to pick them up. "Oh yeah, I picked our birthdays for the mega lotto today. 2- 6- 58 and 12- 1- 61. Why not, you never know," she added, shrugging her shoulders.

"I'll cross my fingers, ha-ha," Dad said, smiling. Mom stepped toward him and kissed him goodbye.

"We'll be back whenever, see you later Hun," Mom exclaimed. We stepped outside and headed to the car.

"Bye babe... see ya Seth. Everything will work out, okay?" Dad shouted from the porch. We turned and waved. Then Dad went inside and shut the door.

Mom and I got in the car and headed to the hospital. It was about a fifteen-minute drive. We listened to the local classic rock station most of the way.

After we checked in, it seemed to take an eternity for us to get called back to a room. The nurses were all nice, but aren't they supposed to be? I think it's part of their job description.

The doctor finally came in and sat down. "What's the reason for your visit today, Seth?" he said, strapping an aneroid monitor on my wrist.

"Well, to start, I'm having nightmares. I'm still confused and dizzy..."

"Well, those things are ..."

"Hold on! Let me finish," I snapped, watching him take my vitals. (I was tired of being interrupted and told how I should feel. No more! I'm telling *him* how *I* feel.) "I keep seeing things... not just in dreams, but every day it's something else. I'm seeing dead people that aren't dead. I'm seeing the walls melt. I keep seeing Laura's Teddy bear running around the house! I'm going insane!"

The Doctor gave Mom a bizarre glance. Mom looked down at the floor.

"What?!" I shouted. "No more secrets!"

"Who said anything about secrets Hun?" Mom asked.

"The look on your face said so," I accused. "Can I get any medication? Is there something that will help? That's why we're here, right?"

"Will you excuse us for a second?" the doctor asked, as he took the monitor off.

"What? Why?" I opposed, feeling powerless.

He set down the monitor, then casually grabbed my mom's arm and lead her to the hall.

This is bull crap! Why can't he say what he needs to say in front of me? I don't like this. I don't like this at all...

I feel trapped. Nobody cares. I'm going to go home and feel the exact same way, just wait. This was all a waste of time...

The door opened with a groan. They had finished their private conversation.

"Okay Seth, your mother and I have discussed a treatment for you. She's going to be the one who makes sure you're taking it. Two pills a day, one in the morning, one at night," the doctor explained.

"So, what is it?" I asked.

"Pardon?" Dr. Hunt played coy.

"The medication, what is it?" I repeated.

"Well... it's a fairly new medication, similar to what might be prescribed for someone with schizophrenia," he said, almost unsure of himself.

My eyes went wide. "Isn't that different though?" I asked, not trusting his answer.

"Yes but..." he paused. "This will be a trial run. It might work, and it might not. But I have a sense you will be feeling better soon."

What is that supposed to mean?

A look of despair crossed my face. I just wanted to feel normal again.

"Thanks Dr. Hunt," Mom said. "Ready to go?" She turned to me.

"That's it?" I asked.

"That's it," Doctor Hunt repeated.

"Sure then," I said, feeling lost... helpless. I stood up and walked out to the foyer. Mom stopped at the front desk to sign some paperwork. It only took a second, then we were out the door.

We went to the pharmacy and filled my prescription. Then Mom went down the road and pulled into Dunkin' Donuts. "You want a treat?" she asked.

"Sure!" I could never turn down a doughnut. Mom knew I was upset. This was her way of making me feel better. We went inside, Mom held the door for me so I could get in. A pretty girl at the counter asked us what we would like. I had to think for a second... I wanted a doughnut, but they all looked so good.

"How about a bear claw," I said licking my lips. "And a Mountain Dew."

"And a Boston cream," Mom added, as she gave the girl five bucks.

The cashier handed us the doughnuts and soda and told us to have a great day. We went out to the car and devoured the sugar, then sped off.

Mom must have been feeling extra sorry for me. We were only about a mile down the road when she asked me if I'd like to watch a movie at the theatre. I was kind of surprised by her question, she was never that nice. But of course, A movie sounded cool. I didn't get to spend much time with her anyway. Although, she was over-playing the kindness a little. It's one thing to be cared for, but I didn't want to be pitied.

We pulled up and started reading off movies that were playing. "*Children of the Corn V, The X-Files, A Perfect Murder, Bride of Chucky*. Gee isn't there a comedy playing?" I asked, throwing up my arms.

Mom started reading. "*Curse of the Puppet Master, Strangers*... there's blood coming from her eyes in that one," she pointed. "Why so many horror movies?"

"Look Mom, *BASEketball* is playing, with Trey

Parker and Matt Stone, and that Yasmine chick," I laughed.

"Sure, that seems funny... I suppose."

* * *

After the movie, we exited the theater and walked through the lobby. "Thanks Mom, that was hilarious!" I said, walking out of the complex and to the car.

"Yeah, it was surprisingly good. A little raunchy, but..." she didn't finish her sentence. We speed-walked the rest of the way to the car, probably because the parking lot was the size of a football field, and the breeze was cool.

We got in the car and headed for home. I turned the radio back on, quiet this time. The sun had gone down, and it was dusky out. Streetlights were turning on.

After about ten minutes, we pulled into our driveway. Instantly, we saw a half-dozen police cars, and an ambulance at the neighbor's house... where Jason lived.

My dream immediately flashed into my mind. *Zombie Jason...*

We stepped out of the car, and I saw Jason's parents talking to the police. I needed to intrude. I *had* to. So, after struggling to get out of the car, I walked over to them. I could see both of Jason's parents were crying. I crept closer, surveilling everything I could. "Not now," a cop barked at me, holding out his arm.

I looked around, feeling helpless. I didn't see Jason anywhere. I started to think something bad had happened to him. Then another officer grabbed my shoulder and spun me around.

"You Seth?" the officer asked.

"Yes sir," I looked up at him.

"Do you know Jason Fletcher?" he asked, looking me in the eyes.

"Yes. Why... what happened?" I started to picture Jason's face down in the sewer.

"When was the last time you saw him?" the officer asked sternly.

"Um... yesterday. No, the day before." I honestly couldn't remember.

"Well..." he said looking around. "He never came home. Jason is missing."

Ten

"Accusations"
NARRATED BY ARIELLE

I dragged my clothes hamper down the basement stairs. I hated it. I had a fear of falling down the stairs... then face-planting the concrete.

But I got down without a problem, and slid my way to the washing machine, opened the door, and tossed in all my dirty tank tops and some Daisy Dukes. I went to grab the detergent, but it wasn't in its normal spot. *Damn I forgot, I used the last of it the other day...*

"Mom," I yelled up the stairs. "You get more soap for the wash?" She must not have heard me. I hesitantly walked up the stairs, trying to picture what she had carried inside from the store. I could hear her doing dishes in the kitchen. That seemed to be her favorite chore.

I walked up to her. "Hey mom, did you get more laundry soap?"

"Oh, yes. I never put it away." Mom started drying her hands on a towel. "Um, over there by the table," she said, pointing to a few bags of groceries still on the floor.

"Thanks Mom," I said cheerfully. I was trying to be extra nice to her. She had been quiet ever since Grandma died. Of course, she missed her mom, it was written all over her face.

And after the little incident with Jason last night, she had been even more upset. And I couldn't blame her. I don't think she liked the idea of her little girl being all grown up, but it happens.

I was going to be a senior next year. My parents were teens at one time, and I've heard some of the stories from when they were in high school. They knew how it was.

I guess I expected to be punished more, and maybe I would be later. But for now, I was not allowed to see Jason, or even talk to him on the phone for at least two weeks. I should have been more careful.

I could still picture Jason's face, when my dad busted us. He was scared to death! I'm surprised he hadn't pissed himself!

The water was still filling up in the washer, so I opened the new detergent and poured some into the machine.

"Ahh!" I heard Seth scream from upstairs.

"Great, what's he seeing now," I mocked, kind of savagely. I should have felt bad for the guy. And I did, but there was a sense of resentment. I couldn't explain it, but it burned inside of me. It wasn't a new feeling, but it was getting stronger.

Maybe because in my mind, Seth had always been treated better than me. He always got the first pick. He never got yelled at by Dad. He always received the more expensive clothing... and I'm the *girl* in the family. *He should be happy with stained jeans and holey T-shirts. But I digress...*

I sat still and heard Mom and Seth having a conversation upstairs. He sounded upset. *Maybe he isn't getting better after all...*

That made me think of Jason again. I really, really liked the guy. I hoped he was alright. Maybe he was too embarrassed to go home. Probably afraid to face his dad. I know I would have been. So, I kept telling myself he had gone to a friend's house. (I had to stay optimistic, otherwise, I felt like killing someone...)

I sat the bottle of detergent up on the shelf and bumped into the box of dryer sheets. It fell and landed between the dryer and the wall. "Poop-nuggets," I said, bending over to retrieve the box.

As I lifted it up, and blew off some dust, I noticed something shiny on the floor... wedged between the dryer and the wall. I could barely squeeze my hand in, but still managed to pull out the object... a bloody knife. The paring knife Mom had asked me about... she said it was missing. *This must be what jabbed Dad...*

I knew instantly who the attacker was. I tightened my fists and clenched my jaw.

Do I really want to stop this madness? Maybe it was for the best. But I had to be sure! I couldn't make any more mistakes.

Am I able to control this thing?

Poor Grandma and Spunky. I felt bad, but she had lived a full life, it was time for her to go. And Spunky was just a dumb dog... life goes on. But I had to make sure my instincts were true... one hundred percent positive, before finishing the job.

What if it comes after me? No... it can't.

My mind was swirling. Too many thoughts at once. I shook my head and took a deep breath. Maybe *I'm* going insane...

I hide the bloody knife in my shorts pocket, then casually walked up the stairs and back into the kitchen. Seth was no longer in the room. "Mom, how come I don't resemble you or Dad?" I blurted out. She nearly choked on her own spit.

"Hun, why do you keep asking?"

"Probably because I never get a good answer," I said, narrowing my eyes.

"Arielle, you know better. It's a recessive gene thing," she said, turning back to the sink. "I don't have time for this. I have to..."

"I think you're full of crap!" I slipped.

"Excuse me! You don't talk to me that way! What's gotten into you lately?" she barked, staring at me with those vexed eyes. I stood there and kind of shrugged, then turned away. She was just proving my point. Changing the subject... that's all it was going to take. "I have to run some errands. Will you keep a close eye on your brother?" Mom asked. "I think he's having another bad day."

I went along with her antics. "So, you think he's getting..." I trailed off. "I'm sorry for saying that. You're not full of crap." I tried to sound as sincere as possible. I still didn't believe her, but I wasn't in the mood for a fight... and I didn't want to push my luck either, I hadn't exactly been a *good girl*.

"It's okay, it's been hectic around here," Mom said with a sigh.

"Yeah," I agreed.

"So, will you hang out here for a bit? Watch Seth? I think it's getting worse..." she said, her eyes getting watery. "Yesterday, at Dr. Hunt's... the things Seth said... just didn't make any sense. But I don't think he's like... delusional or anything. He was aware that he was seeing things that weren't real, you know?"

"Yeah... right Mom," I said disingenuously.

I knew she was just trying to change the subject again. It's what she did best. That's when I grabbed an apple off the dining room table, and went up to my room still angry, trying not to show it on my face.

I entered my room and closed the door. I set the

apple down on my dresser, then started to change my clothes to get comfortable.

I realized I still had that bloody knife in my pocket. The blood was dry and crusty, but I didn't care. I took the knife out and shoved it in the corner of my closet, then set a box of CDs on top of it... looking trustworthy. *Saved for later...*

I really needed to renovate and decorate my room. It was so boring. Whoever lived in the room before me had no taste in anything. Tan walls, tan carpet, and a window. Big deal.

I had a few posters on the walls, but it needed more. Some color to start. Paint the walls purple?

Forget that. To be honest, all I could think about was going back up to the attic...

* * *

I was daydreaming about Jason when the doorbell rang. I walked over to my bedroom door and opened it to go check who it was. But Mom beat me to the front door, so I just crept back and eavesdropped.

"Hello ma'am, I'm Officer Nathan Dunn, this is my partner, Officer Elena Foster."

"Hello," Mom said anxiously.

"Is Mr. Lynch home?" Nathan asked.

"Why yes he is..." Mom said looking down.

Just then, Dad came around the corner to see who was at the door.

"Mr. Lynch?" Nathan asked.

"Yes..." Dad responded, his face confused.

Elena interjected. "We just want to ask you a few questions... may we come in?" She was quiet and seemed less threatening than Nathan. She had bright-red hair like mine, it was beautiful looking. She was short, petite and had perfect teeth. Her looks reminded me of... me.

"You two, come down here." Nathan pointed to my brother and I, now standing at the top of the stairs. The officer was tall and handsome, with dark hair and pointy cheek bones. *I wonder if they're a couple...*

I made it to the bottom of the stairs first. Then Nathan glanced at Seth. "What happened to your leg, Son?"

"Ahh... it's a long story," my brother said through gritted teeth. His response made both cops cock their heads sideways like a dog might when you ask it a question it doesn't understand.

"Do any of you know who lives next door?" Nathan asked, gesturing with a head-nod.

"Yes, the Fletchers. Bob, Cindy, and Jason," Dad said very matter-of-factly. "Is there a problem?"

"Cindy Fletcher reported her son Jason missing yesterday," Elena responded. "When was the last time any of you saw him?"

"Cops already told us he was missing... last night," Seth stated.

I suddenly had a bad feeling. My gut turned into

a pretzel and my heart started racing. Dad turned and looked at me with his eyes wide.

"Yes Mr. Lynch?" Nathan asked, looking at Dad. Nathan wasn't stupid. He read my dad's face like a pop-up book.

Dad turned to face him. "Actually yes, he was here yesterday, and I had to throw him out of my house."

"For what?" Nathan asked.

"That's nobody's business..." Dad said quickly.

"Well, what happened after you threw him out of your home?" Nathan asked.

"Then nothing. I carried on with my business. If you're referring to Jason's whereabouts, I didn't see him after that." Dad shrugged his shoulders.

"Well..." Nathan continued. "The problem is Mr. Lynch, no one else has seen him since last night..." he paused. "So far, it seems like *you* were the last one."

Everyone got quiet. Then Mom spoke up. "Well, there has to be an explanation. My husband didn't do anything to that poor kid..."

"I wouldn't say *nothing*," I said under my breath. *Was that a good idea?*

"What's that mean?" Elena asked me.

I could feel my face start to burn. Everyone was looking at me. My dad's eyes were screaming, *don't you dare.*

"Well?" Nathan prodded.

I had to speak the truth. I had no choice. If I lied, they would see right through me. "My dad..." I paused a moment, I was scared. "My dad caught me and Jason... in the shower." I put my head down in shame. Mom started biting her nails nervously. "And then..." I hesitated.

After a long pause, Elena spoke. "You need to tell us what happened Miss."

"Ugh..." I growled. I took a deep breath and proceeded. "Dad kind of grabbed him by the neck, and pushed him against the wall, but it wasn't bad or anything," I said, trying to defend him. Dad made me angry, but I knew he hadn't hurt Jason. I mean... not to the extreme that would cause him to go missing, anyway.

"Where did this altercation occur? Will you show us?" Nathan asked sternly. Dad and I exchanged glances. I don't think Dad wanted them around. "Please," he finished.

Dad led the way, reluctantly, up the stairs and around the corner. He walked into the bathroom. "Right here," he motioned with a sigh.

Both officers walked into the bathroom and carefully examined the area. "That's quite a nice crack in the wall, is this from last night?" Nathan asked, as if he didn't know the answer. I caught Elena staring at me, probably trying to see whether I was being honest or not.

"Yeah," Dad responded.

"And the hole in the wall?" Nathan added.

"Um... that was afterwards... you know, out of frustration. Listen, I didn't hurt the kid, just scared him. He ran out of here... and that was it," Dad took a deep breath. "He probably put his pants on in the hall and ran out the back door. I mean... can you imagine? Put yourself in my shoes," Dad said, looking at Nathan, hoping he had a daughter and could sympathize. I assumed, anyway.

Nathan gave a nod. "Fair enough," he replied.

"Oh, this is Jason's wallet," Dad said, grabbing it off the countertop. "He dropped it when he ran out of here."

"Thank you," Nathan said. "Unfortunately, since you were the last person to see Jason, we have to take you in."

"What?" Dad replied in shock.

"Seriously?" Seth gasped, his jaw dropping.

The officer pulled out a pair of handcuffs. "Place your hands behind your back," Nathan said with a sigh.

"I didn't do anything!" Dad insisted. But it didn't matter what he said at that point.

"Either way... I'm not saying you're guilty," Nathan said. "If we find no evidence in the next forty-eight hours, you'll be free to go." Nathan seemed to regret cuffing Dad, and Elena had the strangest look on her face. She seemed confused by the situation, while trying to maintain her forced smile.

The countenance on my dad's face, however, was that of drear and defeat. He slowly turned around and let Nathan put the cold, steel cuffs on his wrists.

"If you have nothing to hide, then you have nothing to worry about," Nathan added.

"That's a relief!" Dad responded satirically.

He looked at Mom. "I'm so sorry Hun. I'll be back before you know it." He leaned forward to kiss Mom... her eyes were red and swollen from crying. Then they lead Dad outside like a criminal. We followed and stood near the sidewalk.

"What about your dream, Seth? You should tell them," Mom urged, nudging Seth's shoulder.

"No, it'll sound stupid."

"Stupid is as stupid does...!" I cracked.

"Shut it, Arielle!" Mom barked. She turned back to Seth. "If it would help clear your dad's name..."

"What are you talking about?" I chimed.

"Tell her Seth," Mom said.

"I don't know what to say. I mean, it was just a bad dream. I've been having them a lot lately, remember?" Seth stated.

"But what are the odds?" she said with a smirk, her eyes bulging. "The subconscious mind can be a crazy thing. You wouldn't be the first person to see someone's death before it happened," Mom told him.

"See you guys later!" Dad said as Nathan put him in the car.

"Bye Dad," Seth said.

Mom waved. "Bye!" she said and blew him a kiss. Dad got in the back seat, and the door was shut. He looked at us with sad eyes through the glass.

"But what if they find Jason, and find evidence against Dad to put him away forever?" I asked.

"What are you talking about?! You think Dad is guilty? Huh?" Mom cried.

"No, I'm just saying, not everyone is really who they seem to be..."

"Arielle... I can't even *believe* you are saying that!" Mom expressed loudly.

The officers heard our toxic conversation... they came marching back over.

"How do you think *I* feel? He's *my* boyfriend..." I stated, feeling my throat tighten. My vision became blurry from tears.

"Are you folks okay?" Nathan asked. Elena was standing right behind him.

"Sure," Mom said hesitantly. "Seth, tell them your dream... please."

I wiped tears from my eyes, and watched Seth put his head down. I could tell he didn't want to speak. But I guess he knew he had no choice.

"What's this dream about?" Elena asked.

"Okay..." Seth stood there for a moment not

saying anything. "In the dream I saw Jason in the sewer. He wasn't himself... I mean, like he was dead, or a ghost or something," Seth was babbling.

"Well, that doesn't necessarily mean that Jason is actually..." Elena stopped.

"I know," Seth continued. "But he kept saying, *Help me,* and, *Find me,*" he explained, then paused. "Do you think he was really asking for help?"

"It's not the craziest thing I've ever heard," Nathan exclaimed.

Is that supposed to be a compliment?

"I suppose I can let the search teams know what you said. We'll get more dogs out looking for him too. If Jason is around this area, we'll find him." He tipped his hat. "Thanks for the insight," he said with a smirk and walked away.

That sneer... the cop didn't take Seth seriously...

"Have a nice evening," Elena said with a smile. She glanced at Seth and I, then proceeded to follow Nathan to their vehicle.

"Damn, she's so fine looking," Seth whispered, watching her walk away. "Where have I seen her before?"

Eleven
"Kerflooey Leg"
NARRATED BY SETH

Arielle and I watched helplessly as the cops drove away with our dad in the back of the squad car. Mom was crying again. I don't think she fully realized what was going on.

I didn't want to believe Dad had killed someone, it wasn't his character, even if it was his daughter's boyfriend, whom my dad considered a scumbag, or whatever Jason was to my sister.

Arielle told me everything that happened in her daily life, but she had conveniently left out the part about Jason until the last minute. I guess she really wanted to keep him a secret. *She has been acting different lately... hiding something...*

"I don't think Dad did it," I said, looking at Arielle. "He doesn't have it in him." I was expecting she would agree and was also hoping she would be alright. Her countenance suggested otherwise. *Was that fear, or hatred? Angst or abhorrence?* She didn't look sad, which I found to be odd, but I couldn't tell what she was thinking.

I expected her to start sobbing at the news of Jason, but she just got quiet. She shed a few tears, but I could tell, she was thinking heavily about something else. Probably trying to get the image of zombie Jason out of her head.

"Yeah... I know," she said, burning my eyes with her gaze, then turning away. What an odd way to respond, I thought. *Why is she acting so strange?* Was she in denial? Wanting to think there was no way Dad killed the neighbor kid... but in the back of her mind, she believed he did?

Well, at least that's what was spinning around in *my* head. We don't know what happened, but I was convinced Dad wasn't a murderer. We would find out soon enough anyway...

Arielle turned toward the front door, and Mom and I followed her inside.

After our conversation with the cops, that dream wouldn't leave my mind. Jason jumping into the sewer, then chasing after him, only to find out he's the walking dead? Freaking weird. It was a vivid dream for sure... one I will never forget.

Did my subconscious mind somehow predict the imminent future? Is that possible?

He was standing in my room... was it actually him, or his spirit? Or was I just imagining it? *I should gouge my eyes out... that will solve the problem...*

It was around dinner time and my stomach was eating itself. I was starving and it was time to take my medication anyway. *Twice a day with food,* the doc said. Yeah-yeah. I didn't think Mom was in the mood to cook, so I just hobbled into the kitchen to make myself something.

There was some leftover lasagna that Mom had baked the night before. *Or two nights before?* I cut out a chunk and slapped it on a plate. I put it in the microwave that looked like something had exploded inside. *Has anyone ever cleaned this thing?*

Laura came waltzing in, swinging her Teddy bear around again. She set the stuffed bear on the countertop and grabbed a juice box out of the fridge. Then she ran back out of the room, leaving the bear on the counter next to the toaster.

"You," I said pointing to it. Nobody else was around now. "Why do you gotta mess with me?" I asked the bear facetiously. The thing gave me the creeps...

Watching the timer on the microwave, I noticed something on the bear's arm. I walked over to examine it more closely. It wasn't something *on* the arm, it was wood-wool stuffing coming *out* of it.

The Teddy bear looked like it had been torn at. Its shoulder was ripped, and slivers were hanging out. I could see a few tears along the seam of its armpit as well. One of its black leather shoe-button eyes was loose and slightly hanging.

The thing smelled awful, and I could see dark patches where it looked like it had rolled around in the dirt. *Maybe it was in a fight...* the thought was dumb but amusing.

The microwave dinged. My mouth watered from the aroma.

As I pulled the door open, the bear stood up and lunged at me. "Whoa!" I cried out. The bear clung to my throat. It was surprisingly strong. The force of the bear made me lose my balance. I tried to catch myself, but my kerflooey leg flew out from under me. Trying to rip the bears hold free, I fell backward. The bear was trying to strangle me to death.

I started tugging at its torn shoulder, ripping at snarls of wood-wool. The bear was pushing down on my trachea, pinching off my air. I rolled over on my side and pulled harder at its opened wound. I heard the snapping of threads, and a deep tearing sound. *I'm going to rip this arm right off!*

That's when the bear loosened its grip, and I threw the bastard off me. *How is it so strong?*

I reached for my neck, it felt good to breathe again. I looked up to make sure the bear wasn't coming back for me... but I couldn't see it anywhere.

I managed to pull myself to my feet, using the counter for balance. *Where did the bear go?*

"Mom, Arielle, somebody!" I yelled. What had just happened? I couldn't focus on anything. The room was spinning. Then I saw Mom run into the kitchen.

"S'tahw gnorw traehteews?" I saw her mouth move, but nothing made sense.

I cupped my hands over my ears and bent over screaming. *I'm going insane... I can't take this anymore! Why does this happen every time? I'm going to snap!*

Mom put her hands on my shoulders, trying to calm me down.

"Seth- Seth... Hun, relax..." she said, squeezing my arms.

I felt myself shaking all over. Letting myself fall to the floor, I curled into a ball, and started rocking back and forth. I focused on the wall, and nothing else.

"What happened now?" Mom asked with a worried look on her face.

"I don't know..." I said feeling helpless.

"Seth, what do you mean you don't know?"

I remained there for a moment, feeling embarrassed. I didn't want to tell her what I had just seen. I just wanted to be set free from this. "Okay..." I started. *I might as well spit it out, she won't leave me alone until I do.* "So, I was nuking lasagna and Laura came in with her Teddy bear. I went for my food... and the thing attacked me!"

Mom looked at me strangely, which was expected. "When I finally got the stupid thing off me, it must have run away. I didn't see where it went."

"It wasn't real sweetheart," Mom reassured me. She took her hand and messed up my hair.

"Yes, it was! I can still feel it pushing down on my throat. It was losing its stuffing from one arm. I saw it!" I buried my head in my hands and sighed.

Mom just looked at me with a blank glaze over her eyes. "So... where did the bear go?"

"I already told you... I don't know. It ran off somewhere," I said in desperation.

"And who's Teddy bear is it again?" Mom asked, lowering her voice.

Didn't I just explain myself? I was quite sure I already had...

"Laura... it's Laura's bear. She's the one that brought..."

"Seth... *who* is Laura?" Mom interrupted.

"U-uhm..." I started trembling all over. "Your... your daughter! My little sister..." I roared, feeling deflated on the inside.

Mom looked at me with sadness. "Oh no," she said softly, putting her head down. "Seth... there is no Laura."

* * *

Lying in bed that night, I couldn't fall asleep. I tossed and turned, I even tried counting sheep, but nothing was working.

I wasn't sure if I even wanted to sleep. My reality and my nightmares were blending... or one was crossing over into the other... couldn't be sure. But I was afraid of losing the ability to tell them apart. *Maybe I should stay awake...*

My mom's words were repeating in my head. They were haunting me, *there is no Laura... there is no Laura...* and that made me start questioning everything. For example, how is it that when I saw Laura, it felt like she had always been around? I think my brain had developed false memories of her. There was no other way to explain it...

When was this medication supposed to start working anyway? *Whatever... they are probably sugar pills...*

Doctors only care about money. They could care less if I got better, (as long as their wallets get fatter that is). *Just fill the script. Next...*

That's from my experience anyway. I was reminded of a time I went to the *local-care* clinic. The doctor lied through his teeth just to get me out as fast as possible. *Make that money, screw the people...*

He literally ignored my diagnosis and made up his own. Then prescribed meds I didn't need. That's sick... and not in the good way. Seriously, get a life! He wouldn't even look me in the eyes. *Make that money, screw the people...*

I don't see doctors anymore unless it's out of my

control. Maybe that's not fair to the people who *do* care, but they are the minority.

My mind was zooming. I wondered what Sue had been up to. *Skank*. Ditching me for some other dude because I was laid up for a few days. Pfft... who needed that kind of abuse. Why did I even think about her anymore? It was obvious I cared more for her than she did for me... *I hope everything goes back to normal, life as usual... everything... back to normal...*

I allege I fell asleep because a loud discord jolted me awake. I sat straight up in bed, and heard that noise again, coming from the attic. What *is* that? I decided it was time to find out.

I slid out from my covers, grabbed my cane, and inched my way to the door. I walked quietly. I didn't want anyone else to hear me. I cracked open my door and crept out.

The attic's pull-down stairs were in the hallway, between my bedroom door and Arielle's. The stairs were closed, but the rope dangling from them was swaying. Someone was already up there...

I decided to look in Arielle's room first. I slowly crept my way past the swinging rope. Floorboards were squeaking under my good leg, which held most of my weight. Lights from a passing car outside rolled against the wall.

When I got close, I saw Arielle's door ajar, so I peeked in. It was dark at first, but my eyes slowly adjusted. I could see that her bed was empty. Bingo! Then I thought, who else would it be? Mom or Dad in the middle of the night? Unlikely.

I turned back around and made my way to the attic. As I approached, the stairs started to come down. I took a few steps back and watched from a distance. My knees started to feel weak.

When the glorified ladder touched down, Arielle started climbing to the floor. It was dark but I could see the design on her pajamas. She held the Teddy bear in one arm.

"Arielle? What are you doing up there?"

"Ahh," she gasped. "You scared the hell out of me! What are you doing out here?"

"I asked you first," I said, looking at the bear. Then I backed up some more. "What the hell are you doing with that thing?"

"It's none of your business," she railed.

"That bear tried to kill me," I said, half believing myself. She didn't respond. "Well... can't you at least tell me what you were doing in the attic?"

"Again... none of your beeswax," she said rolling her eyes.

"You're not acting like yourself, Arielle."

"*I'm* not acting like myself... right. At least I'm not a schizophrenic psychopath!" she wailed in a harsh whisper.

Her words stabbed me in the heart. I was taken aback and felt a lump form in my throat.

Could she really feel that way? I didn't even do anything... none of this was my fault! I was in the wrong place at the wrong time. How dare she!

"You have problems, you know that?" I jeered, my mouth feeling dry.

"You have no idea," she shot back harshly, pushing the stairs back into the ceiling. Then without saying another word, she walked down the hall, into her bedroom and closed the door.

Twelve
"Territorial Pissings"
NARRATED BY SEAN LYNCH

I spent the night in jail. It wasn't the most pleasant experience of my life. The mattress I slept on was more like a hammock, all indented and concave. My cell smelled like a toilet and an ashtray. The meal they served was better than a microwave dinner, so that was a plus... but I don't want to go back. No way.

I'm just glad they found Jason. Well... not exactly glad. They found his body in the middle of the night, in the sewer. I can't even imagine how he ended up down there. Poor kid. I wanted to hurt him before, seeing him with my daughter and all, but I felt bad for the guy. He didn't deserve that. And as hard as it seemed, I felt bad for Jason's family, even his unfriendly father.

So, I was relieved when the guards came to me and said I could go home. Jason's body had decomposed badly. Worse than normal, I heard, because of the condition he was left in. The water, rats, and bacteria made it hard to identify him.

When I was being questioned, I remembered I had taken twenty bucks from Jason's wallet and went to the hardware store downtown. *I didn't tell them I took the money.* I just wanted some duct tape and a new variety pack of Phillips bits for my drill. I told the detectives what hardware store I had gone to. I had wandered through a couple different aisles, and as it checked out, they had me on camera. The time stamp on the video showed I was there around the same time Jason went missing. So that worked out in my favor. I was so relieved they had evidence of my innocence.

My arresting Officer Dunn said he would escort me to my house. On the drive to my place, Nathan asked me about my son's leg. I told him the story of how he was in an accident with another police officer. He found it sort of ironic. Then he asked me about Seth's dream.

"He never mentioned it to me," I responded, shaking my head. "I don't remember any dream."

"Yeah, you were already in the back seat of my car when he told me last night," he added.

I nodded. "So, what exactly did he tell you?" I was curious after all.

"Well, ah..." Nathan started. "He said he saw Jason in the sewer... all messed up... that Jason talked to him and was asking for help," he paused. "I'd have to say, that's a new one for me." *Did he just suggest my son was crazy?*

"Well, he suffered a major concussion because of the accident. He's been having a hard time," I said, trying to defend my son.

"Oh yeah... I've seen all kinds," Nathan added. *What the hell was that supposed to mean? Do I have to knock this cop out?*

He pulled into my driveway, and we stepped out. I was a little irritated at how Nathan was acting... almost accusatory, but mostly sarcastic. I kept telling myself to shut up, and he would be gone soon.

I ran into the house and found Seth watching TV. "Hey Seth."

"Dad! Hey, I didn't know you'd be home so soon?" He stood up. I walked over and gave him a hug.

"Of course I'd be home," I chuckled. "Where's everyone else?" I asked.

"Mom and Arielle went shopping, said they would be gone for a few hours."

"They couldn't wait?" I asked rhetorically. "Anyway, come outside for a minute, that cop Nathan is outside, he wants to talk to you a sec."

"Really? About what?" he asked, hopping on one foot.

"I don't remember. Oh... he mentioned a dream... something about a dream. Sorry, he made me angry," I confessed.

"Zombie Jason," he belched inappropriately.

I just shook my head. *Sometimes he has quite the imagination...*

We both wandered outside. Nathan was still standing by his vehicle.

Seth wobbled over with his cane in one hand, pushing up on the ground, helping to balance himself.

"Seth," Nathan started. "We spoke yesterday..."

"Yes sir, I remember," he said.

"Good. So, about your friend there, Jason. Do you have any idea how he ended up in the sewer?"

"Not a clue," Seth responded.

"But you had that dream, right? And you saw where he was?" Seth nodded his head. "Were there any more details you forgot to mention?" Nathan asked.

"No, not that I can think of," Seth paused a moment. "In the dream he jumped in the sewer on his own..."

"Well, I don't think that's what happened," Nathan said, assuming foul play.

"It wasn't me," Seth started. "I was with my mom at the hospital when Jason went..."

"I know Seth, I know. I was already informed. You guys seem like a nice family," the officer said, trying to clear his throat. "The lab found mohair on him, which they told me was strange, because it comes from the Angora goat that lives in Asia. I didn't even know what an Angora was but..." Nathan stopped. "Can I get a glass of water?" he asked, trying to clear his throat again.

"Sure, you want a bottle?" I asked running inside. I grabbed a cold bottle for him and went back out. "Here you are, don't choke on it," I said, being an ass.

Without saying a word, Nathan reached out his arm and grabbed it. He opened the bottle and chugged. Then he made an obnoxious satisfying grunt.

"Ahh, that's better," he said. "So, they don't know where the mohair came from. Coroner's office said Jason was in a struggle. He had slashes on his abdomen, a broken leg, and plenty of other antemortem injuries. He had lacerations on his face and arms. I can't go into much more detail but..." he trailed off. "It seems like... he was taken by surprise. Someone had it out for the kid. They're going to open an investigation. You should expect more visits..."

"Oh great," I threw in.

"You all have a good day," Nathan said as he turned to leave.

"I'm glad your home Dad," Seth told me, smiling.

"Me too... me too." I gave him another hug.

"I'm going to clean up, I smell like an armpit's asshole," Seth joked.

"Nice one! Don't fall and break your other leg," I said being a smart-ass.

Seth disappeared upstairs to get cleaned up. It was nice to see him smile for a change, and it felt good to be home. I started to wonder about Bob and Cindy next-door. They must have been having a difficult time... I couldn't even imagine. I should have done something nice for them, but then again, Bob was as predictable as the weather. The thought made me uneasy. Why couldn't I have normal neighbors? People that wanted to play horseshoes or euchre and drink some beers, grill some steaks over charcoal... those kinds of people. But no...

A ruffling sound from the kitchen made me jump. Then I heard the trash receptacle fall over. It's an unmistakable sound, with the dog getting into old food scraps, I've heard that sound many times. But Spunky was no longer with us...

I sat up and walked into the kitchen. As I predicted, the trash was strewn about. Trying to understand what had just occurred, I felt as if I was being watched. I could feel eyes on me. But from where? *And who tipped this garbage over?*

I flipped the plastic receptacle back in place and started picking up the mess. The feeling of eyes staring at me grew stronger. I stood up and examined my surroundings. I gazed in every direction, in the corners, out the windows... I kept still for a moment and listened. *This is nuts... whatever. There's nobody here...*

I needed a distraction, so I grabbed up the trash and walked outside.

* * *

Allison and Arielle were still out shopping, I decided it was a good time to fix the gutter out back. I think it detached itself during the wintertime. I'm not sure exactly how, but suddenly it started pissing water all over the deck when it rained. Kind of defeated the purpose of the thing.

After I tossed the garbage away, I walked around to the garage. I needed a ladder and probably some hand tools. Inside, I walked over to the dark corner and hoisted the ladder up. I spun it around and headed out of the garage. I squeezed in between the house and my truck, trying not to smash my headlights with the ladder base. Our swimming pool came into view. *I should take the cover off and jump in... that would be refreshing...*

As I was setting up the ladder in the correct position, I saw Bob charge out his front door, and start walking right toward me. I could imagine he believed I was the individual responsible for his son's disappearance. If I were him, I would have thought the same thing. After all, we are only human. *I hope he doesn't start anything...*

So, I headed back to the garage for a couple screw drivers, tin snips, and some sealant.

I was reaching for my snips when Bob's shadow appeared on the wall. I did a quick 180° and saw him standing by my truck. He was wearing a wifebeater and had a wooden baseball bat in his hand, trying to look tough I assumed. Though he didn't need any help looking scary. His eyes were narrowed to a point. His forehead had those angry creases, and I saw his nostrils flare.

He's going to kill me...

"Bob, what brings you over here?" I asked, my voice shaky.

"I think you already know," he said menacingly.

"Uh... Bob..." I started walking along the wall, trying to creep out of the garage. "If this is about your son..."

"Your damn right it's about my son!" he screamed, taking a few more steps. I started making my way closer to the driveway. I figured being out in the open would be the safest place from this maniac.

"I have kids too," I started. "Listen... I wouldn't do anything to hurt your kid, I promise."

"Cops told me you choked my son, right before you threw him out of your house..." Bob accused, raising the bat above his head.

"Well now, I..."

-Smash-

Shards of glass from my passenger window went flying in all directions. Bob stood there breathing heavily. I was scared, and desperately wanted to escape the garage. "Bob, you don't understand..."

"You killed my son!" he wailed, charging at me, raising the bat again. I leaped back and the bat connected with my truck's side mirror. It flew off with a crunch and landed in the middle of my driveway.

"Bob, listen... I didn't kill your son! I'm sorry I put my hands on him, but he had his hands on my daughter!" I figured showing some aggression would make him back off...

I was wrong. He swung the bat again, aiming for my head. I raised my arm to shield. The bat struck me with a cracking sound. Pain shot up my arm to my spine. Bob raised the bat once again and sucker-jabbed me in the ribs.

"Ah... damnit Bob!" I fell to the floor, holding my body.

"Get up!" Bob screamed. He looked down at my truck, then proceeded to smash out my headlights. "Get up," he repeated.

"I'm home Bob, think about it... I'm not in jail because..." I stopped to catch my breath. "I had an alibi... I'm on tape at the... at the hardware store... you have to believe me..." I pleaded, cowering.

Bob could have killed me if he really wanted to. But I think he started to realize the verity of the situation. He knew I didn't kill Jason. That didn't mean he still wasn't an upset father. And he knew killing me for revenge, or out of rage, wouldn't solve anything.

"Bob, you don't have to do this you know... we can talk about this... we can work things out. If you need someone to confide in..."

"Shut up!" he screamed. He threw the bat against the wall and walked away. Containers of nails and screws fell and clanged onto the floor. Bob strolled through the yard, looking defeated. Before he reached his house, I watched him rip out chunks of his hair and scream, this time hunched over.

* * *

There I sat, in the garage, on my ass, and just stared at my busted-up truck. My arm was already black and blue, and my ribs felt fractured. But I guess it could have been worse...

I lit a cigarette and took a big drag.

That son of a bitch ruined my truck. Did I have it coming? I didn't think so. I reacted the way any father would have, right?

It's too late to change anything now...

I can't believe it. How am I supposed to pay for all this? A new window, lights, mirror. Damnit! That guy gets under my skin. I should go over there right now and destroy *his* truck... or slice off his valve stems in the middle of the night. Yeah, that'll teach the prick!

But deep down, I knew I wouldn't do it. Enough

has occurred already. Why make things worse...

I finished smoking and put the butt in the can by the wall. I figured I should continue what I started and fix the leaky gutter. I was pretty sure it had separated at the seam... an easy fix.

It was such a nice day out. The perfect temperature, a nice little breeze and birds chirping all around. The best time of year.

I had a screwdriver in one pocket, sealant in the other, and carried the snips in my hand while climbing the ladder. As I pulled myself up, my arm twinged in pain, reminding me of Bob's baseball bat. *He's gonna get his... one day.*

I reached the top rung and used the roof as a tool bench. I examined the gutter and saw that it was just as I had suspected. In the corner was a little hole. I reached into my pocket for the sealant.

A strong breeze made me wobble on the ladder and I almost lost my balance. My heart started beating fast. I had to tell myself to calm down.

I opened the sealant and squeezed some goop in the hole. With a shop rag I wiped up the remaining gunk and made it look nice. "Easy," I told myself.

That was all it took... a job well done. I reached for my tin snips and took a step down on the ladder. Then I felt a heavy force on my legs... like the ladder had been shoved.

That must be exactly what happened. The next thing I knew, I was falling backward. I tried to grab onto the roof, but it was already out of reach. I swung my arms in the air, then turned and jumped off the ladder... just in time to fall on top of the pool tarp.

I started to sink... water started splashing up all around. Then a wave crashed over me, and I went under. I was trying to pick my head up, but I was getting tangled in the tarp. It felt like the tarp was dragging me under, pulling me like some kind of hungry sea creature.

I started to panic... I was running out of air. I kicked my legs and thrashed my arms, trying to pull myself to the surface. My lungs started to ache and feel tight. Nothing seemed to be working. *I need air!*

I gave one more push of desperation. *Oh God please help me! I can't breathe!*

I couldn't tell what was right-side up anymore. I felt myself drifting, then my limbs went limp, and everything faded away...

Thirteen
"Gut Instinct"
NARRATED BY ARIELLE

When Mom and I came home from shopping, there were cops in our driveway. Seth was holding himself up with a crutch, standing in the front yard. His eyes were all red and puffy. My gut started to tie itself in knots. I had a bad feeling.

Mom put the car in park, and quickly got out. "Seth what's going on?" she yelled.

"It's Dad, he had an ac..." Seth could barely speak... he was sobbing too hard. "An accident..."

I wrapped my arms around him tightly.

"Where's your father?" Mom asked him. That made Seth start crying harder. I was starting to think the worst.

Then a man I recognized came over in his uniform. "Officer Dunn!" Mom shouted. "Where's my husband?"

"Hi again," Nathan said. "There's no easy way to say this... I'm so sorry ma'am. It seems that Seth here found your husband in the pool in your backyard."

"What...?" Mom sighed, looking desperate.

"It looks like he drowned. I'm so deeply sorry." Nathan put his head down, showing sincerity.

"Oh...!" Mom collapsed on the ground.

"Looks like an accident," he continued. "We'll know more after an autopsy."

Mom started to wail like I had never heard in my life. Her cries sent shivers down my spine. I went over to comfort her, but my effort was futile. She was a wreck, and it seemed like nothing would help. Life was getting flipped upside down, and gravity took a vacation.

Watching her suffer like that was hard. It was much harder on Seth than me. He was still sniffling, with a lost, blank stare on his face. I don't know what was harder for him... Dad's death, or watching Mom weep over him...

Nathan asked if there was anything else he could do to help. I just shook my head.

They took Dad away in a body bag. Black and dull... the stinging sight of death. The air was moist and no longer seemed refreshing. The sun was beginning to set, the light was being extinguished. Darkness was taking over.

When the ambulance drove away with Dad, the three of us watched until it was out of sight. Time had seemed to slow down. We stood there in silence for a few more minutes. Then with nothing left to stare at, we went inside.

Mom didn't talk the rest of the night. She didn't do anything except cry, and leer at the wall. Poor Mom. Eventually she stood and went upstairs. I just assumed she was going to bed. What else was there to do at a time like this?

Seth was watching TV. At least his eyes were, I could tell his mind was far away. Between Dad, and everything else that's happened recently, I think Seth wanted to check out. He looked lost. His eyes were gone.

I've never seen someone so screwed up before. I mean seriously. He's a mental case. His fault or not, he belongs in a home.

"Sorry Seth," I said, looking up at him. I noticed his eyes were closed now. "I hope you can forgive me... goodnight brother," I whispered.

* * *

The next morning came too soon. I had a feeling it would be an eventful day. I was already nervous, my heart racing, and I had only been awake for thirty seconds. *Maybe a hot shower will calm me down a bit...*

I made the water as hot as I could tolerate, and jumped in. Washing my hair, I started thinking about Dad. Seeing his lifeless body... it made me cringe. I started to feel my chest get tight, but I forced myself to relax. Stop dwelling on the past, I scolded myself. *I can't be upset. I must keep it together...*

The water against my back felt good, but despite this, my mind was racing... I soaped up and rinsed off in record time.

I turned off the water, shoved the curtain aside, and reached for my towel. I moved my hand along the wall, feeling for the rack... but the towel wasn't where I left it. *Now that I think about it, I can't remember seeing it...*

Assuming it had fallen, I reached down and felt along the floor for my towel. When I found it, I brought it up to dry my face, but something was wrong. It felt warm and slimy and smelled awful. "*Pew,*" I cracked in shock. *What the hell is that?*

I threw the towel down on the floor and started reaching blindly for the handles to turn the shower back on. I shoved my face in the water, removing the slime.

Then, out of curiosity, I scooped the water out of my eyes and glanced at the towel on the floor. It was covered in... *is that blood? What?* It looked like an animal's entrails had been put in a blender, then served on my towel. A hot wave of nausea crashed over me.

The smell of death wouldn't leave my nostrils. I washed my hair and face again to get the funk off me. At first, I was furious, but I knew it was my fault. Just some baggage, I told myself. Not every plan works out perfectly. *Like a cat, leaving a mouse by the door... a pleasant little gift.*

I finally hopped out of the tub and walked dripping wet to the linen closet. I grabbed a clean towel and wrapped it around myself. The sunlight coming in through the window was beaming in the steamy bathroom air. I grabbed a garbage bag from under the sink and shoved the massacred towel in, then walked to my room to get dressed. I tossed the garbage bag in the corner to take outside later. *Disgusting...*

I could hear Mom in the kitchen, probably cooking up some grub. The shower had helped, but I was still feeling jittery. I went downstairs and saw Seth in his favorite chair eating some cereal. "Good morning," I said feeling refreshed.

Seth put his head down and grunted... then he popped his head back up. "What did you say?" he asked, looking confused.

"I asked how you were doing?"

"Oh... I'm alive, I guess," he answered. He was scooping up cereal, then letting it plop back into his bowl. There were drops of milk splattered all over the table.

"Morning Hun," Mom greeted. It was good to see her cheerful. "Want some eggs?" she asked.

"Maybe later," I responded. I had too much on my mind to eat. I was surprised I even slept well.

When will I put an end to this?

A car horn from outside made me jump. Seth

stood up and started walking to the front door.

"Where are you going Hun?" Mom asked.

"Gonna hang with the guys for a little while... the usual," he replied dismally. I could see some worry on Mom's face.

"Be safe Seth, I love you," Mom added. Seth smiled and then went out the door.

The questions kept nagging me. They wouldn't leave me alone. I had to get the answers. Knowing the truth was my priority for the day. And I knew, today would be the last time I would ask...

* * *

I poured myself a glass of orange juice, the real stuff, not orange flavored drink, and started nervously pacing back and forth. Mom must have noticed I was stressed out. "What's on your mind Hun?" she asked. I finished my glass and set it on the counter. I stood a moment thinking. *It's now or never...*

"Mom, have you ever studied genetics?" I asked nonchalantly. Mom waited a moment to respond.

"Where are you going with this?" she asked suspiciously.

"I was just wondering," I lied.

Mom came over and sat at the table with a plate of scrambled eggs and toast. It smelled awful. It always made the kitchen smell dirty to me. More so when she cooked bacon. I know... weird.

"Actually, I've been doing some research," I

said, trying to be clever. She looked up at me with her high-strung eyes, but only for a moment. "Remember Seth's party, when Dad got hurt?"

"Yeah... why do you ask?" she retorted.

"Because I found the knife that stabbed him."

"I didn't know it was a knife that did it," she replied, acting like she didn't care, her voice monotone.

"It sure was, and I had the blood tested," I snarked.

"Huh?" she responded nervously.

"Yeah, I was joking when I told Dad I could give him some of my blood, just to humor him. But his response wasn't normal, and I just couldn't let it go. The look on his face... he had to be acting that way for a reason... and I think it's the same reason I look nothing like any of you!" I started to raise my voice. "I'm not that stupid."

"I never said you were stupid Hun," Mom said, avoiding my eyes.

"Quit calling me Hun! Who's my real mother? Do you know? Who is she!"

Mom looked shocked and nearly fell over backward. "I'm your mother. I've taken care of you your whole life!"

"But you weren't the one who gave birth to me... right? Or am I wrong?" I crossed my arms. She stood there quietly. "That's what I thought," I continued. "The blood on the knife was *A-negative*.

And my blood is *AB-positive*. My blood would *kill* Dad. You know what that means don't you?" I asked impertinently.

Her countenance changed, and she put on her defensive face. "Why can't you just let things go? Don't you have a good life? Just stop already..." she huffed.

My face got flush. "I did have a good life, but if everything is a lie... can it be good anymore?"

"Yeah, it can be good," Mom said. "You should be happy, but instead you're this selfish little brat, who never knows what's good for her!"

"Oh, shut up *Mom!*" I was getting angry. I could feel the veins in my forehead pulsing. Then a thought came to me... "You know who my real mother is, don't you?"

She sat there silently. The lack of a response... was a response. That made the rage spill over inside me. The room felt like it was spinning. "Who is she?!" I screamed at her. "Who?"

"I guess it doesn't matter anymore, so..." she began. "Your mother lives in the next town over. Her real name is Bella Rosalind," she explained.

I sat there in shock for a moment. I couldn't believe what I was hearing. "I don't get it?" I said, feeling excited and lifeless, all at once.

"That's why we moved here... Bella is my cousin sweety," she explained.

"Okay... What does that have to do with me?" I

asked.

"Okay. I'm just going to start from the top," she said with a heavy sigh.

"That would be nice..." I said sharply.

She took a deep breath. "Your mom was raped when she was fourteen. She loved you so much, but... she couldn't take care of you. I'm a few years older than her... and I had just given birth to Seth at the time. One night we talked for hours... and I finally agreed to take you... and raise you."

"What the... seriously?" I trembled.

"It was only supposed to be temporary. You don't understand," she started to cry. "I've been bugging her all these years, telling her she needed to reach out to you... to tell you the truth. But the longer she waited, the harder it became. She's afraid now. It's been so long, she's afraid you will hate her, or reject her."

"No, no... I want to know my mother, not an imposter!" I wailed.

"Please Hun, don't be upset with me. We did what we thought was right, we really did." She paused. "Bella said it was finally time to meet you properly... that's why we moved. Your mom is only a few minutes away," she said, wiping tears off her face.

"So, my mom... she plans on finding me? I don't get it."

"Oh, no, she knows where we live. She was here

the other night. The red-headed cop?" she explained, her eyes getting wide.

"Wait-wait-wait... you mean to tell me... my real mother was here? Right in front of me? And nobody mentioned it?" I asked furiously. I was face to face with her, and never even knew...

Sadness overwhelmed me, knowing I had missed the opportunity. My Mom was here! I had known for years something was wrong... a reason I didn't fit in.

But now... I was feeling stabby.

"I'm sorry," she said. "Put yourself in my shoes. I didn't know what to do... I was under the impression that she would eventually be your mother... that one day she would come around," Mom retorted.

Maybe I shouldn't call her Mom anymore... I was just so used to it. But that had to change. *From now on, I will call her Allison...*

"Seriously? That's your best excuse?" I wailed. "You lied to me my whole life!"

"It was for *your* benefit Arielle! What else was I supposed to do? And it wasn't all my idea... your mom and I planned it together."

"I hate you!" I shouted, shoving her as hard as I could.

She stumbled backward. "How dare you push me!" she yelled as she took a few steps closer. Then she got in my face, so I pushed her again. "Get your hands off of me!" she screeched... then charged at me, slamming her body into mine. I went sailing through the air and fell into the dish rack. I tumbled to the ground. Ceramic plates went crashing to the floor, shattering to pieces. Knives and silverware fell out, splashing all over the kitchen.

I saw red... and did the only thing I could. I picked myself up and grabbed a steak knife from the floor... and charged back at Allison. I screamed as I leaped at her... and drove the knife into her gut. Then I pulled the blade out... and stabbed harder. A woosh of air escaped her lips. Then I pushed her over, and she fell on her back, thudding hard on the floor. She gurgled... the knife sticking out of her body.

Allison looked at me wide-eyed. Her face was saying, *how could you...*

She spit up some blood and squeaked. "I loved you like... like a... daughter."

"Oh well," I said harshly.

"That's just... like you... thinking... only of... yourself," she said with short breaths, her voice getting quiet... the color running from her face.

"I don't care anymore... that should be obvious by now," I said with authority.

I left Allison bleeding on the floor and walked over to the stove. I blew out the pilot lights and turned all four burners on high...

Fourteen
"The End"
NARRATED BY SETH

Ed had picked me up, and we went over to Jeff's house to check out a game on his *PlayStation*. We were playing *NASCAR '98*. It was sick! There's a cheat code where you can shoot paintballs from your car! It destroys everyone... cars would start crashing and flipping... lots of fun.

We played more games for a while, but I wasn't exactly in the mood. I was using the game time as an excuse... I couldn't stop thinking about Dad, and everything else peculiar that was happening.

After about an hour I was getting the munchies. I asked Ed to drive me home. He insisted on going to the gas station for *Little Debbie* snacks, but I wanted real food. I couldn't fill up on sugar all the time.

So, Ed and Jeff dropped me off at home.

"Peace dude," Ed said, as they pulled away. I gave a quick wave and started slowly walking to the front door.

When I stepped foot inside, Arielle was there to greet me. "Hello brother," she said, startling me.

"Whoa, damn..." I said, throwing my cane down on the floor. "You scared the crap out of me," I admitted. She just looked at me with this strange smirk. "Why are you standing here in the dark?" I asked, looking around. It was quiet. All the lights were off. The drapes and windows were closed...

"I just wanted to welcome you home," she said smiling.

"Since when...?" I asked, my stomach growling. "I need some food."

"Ha-ha, Good luck with that," Arielle snarked. *What the hell does that mean?* I gave her a weird look and marched to the kitchen. A peanut butter and jam sandwich sounded good.

That's when I smelled gas. I took a few more steps into the kitchen and saw Mom, lying on her back in a pool of her own blood. Broken plates and silverware decorated the floor.

"Mom!" I shrieked and fell to my knees. I crawled over to her. "Mom!" She was lifeless. There was nothing I could do to save her. "Why!" I cried. "Mom, why, why...!"

What is left for me? What am I supposed to do now?

"She had an accident," Arielle said, walking into the room. "I had to teach her a lesson."

"What the hell does that mean? You did this?" I

asked.

"Yours truly," she answered with a curtsy.

"You're a psycho!" I lashed out. She seemed to ignore my cry.

"I have someone who wants to say hi," she said pointing. I sat up in a sitting position to see what Arielle was talking about. That's when Teddy came running up to me, carrying a knife.

"Huh?" I cried out in shock. Teddy took a dive at me, and I hunched back. Teddy sank the knife deep in my leg... my good leg. "Ahh, damnit!" I cried out in pain. The bear pulled the knife out. "Get away!" I shouted, shoving the bear aside. Then it swung the blade at my throat. I blocked it with my arm, getting it sliced in the process. Blood dripped onto my pants.

"That's enough," Arielle commanded, then said a word I didn't recognize. The bear backed away.

I tried to stand up, but I was in too much pain. My leg was throbbing now. Arielle came over and boot-stomped me in the face... making sure I wasn't going to move. "Don't be in such a hurry," she sneered.

I went limp and saw stars. I laid on my back, my head flopping from side to side. I grabbed my face, my nose felt broken. Against my better judgment, I struggled to bring myself back to a sitting position. "Why would you do that?" I asked, tasting blood in my mouth. My lips quivered. "What are you doing?

Have you lost your mind?" Blood dripped from my face to my lap.

"I think I finally found my mind... I was naive before, but now it's all so clear..." Her speech faded away.

More questions were flooding my mind. "What's up with the bear? How are you doing that?" I asked, spitting blood and phlegm on the floor.

"Haha, I thought you would never ask," she started. "He's my little apprentice. I can't have blood on my hands."

"Except Mom's," I provoked.

"Shut your face! If you know what's good for you," she snapped. "Teddy bears don't leave behind fingerprints, or DNA... so it works out."

"So, like... this is your plan?" I asked.

"Plan? Not really. It's more like... a timely opportunity," she said. "Honestly... at this point I'm just improvising," she added with a sinister chuckle.

The smell of the gas was starting to make me dizzy and feel sick to my stomach. My heart was racing, and my skin was getting clammy. From the look on her face, she was having the same problem.

"I found Teddy in the attic. He was holding a book... and it told me everything about the dark arts," Arielle explained, pacing back and forth. "I learned how to bring Teddy to life. And now... he does *my* bidding."

"I still don't understand..."

"When Teddy killed Spunky, and then Jason, I thought I should try to put it back to sleep. They didn't deserve to die. But then I read more of the book, and my power over Teddy grew." She turned to look at me. "Spunky and Jason were just a bump in the road."

"You killed Jason?" I asked, knowing the answer. "What about Grandma?"

"Take a look at my face! Do I look anything like you? *Brother*," she inserted sarcastically. "I was adopted, Mom and Dad lied about it... our whole lives Seth!" I saw a tear run down her cheek. "But now I know who my real mother is. I'm going to start over... a new life. And I'm not leaving any evidence behind."

"You're crazy! You're just a modern-day witch!" I accused, still sitting on the floor. "There is no way you'll get away with this!" I shouted.

"Oh... but I already have Brother... I already have."

"You have nowhere to go if you blow the place," I said, knowing her intentions.

"I'm *hot* remember... you don't think I could find a sugar-daddy to take care of me? Please..." she laughed.

I couldn't believe what I was hearing. My heart was galloping, the room spinning. I was in pain and could hardly move. I spit some more blood onto the floor.

I should try to stop her... before she blows the place to hell...

"Os, m'I annog evael," Arielle said.

I started pulling at my hair. "Please God, not now!" I choked out. *This can't be happening to me now!*

"Yeh esactun... uoy ereht?"

I need to focus. Come on... focus!

I started to sway back and forth. The pressure in my head wouldn't stop.

It's all in your head...

"What?" I asked, trying to understand.

"I said I'm going to leave now!" she screamed. I realized my cognition recommenced. "It was nice knowing you Seth... I'm going to miss ya," she added, her voice suddenly calm.

"Yeah... right..." I snarked, shaking my head. The room stopped spinning on me. Then I realized I had forgotten to take my pill this morning.

"I gave Teddy a box of matches. He's rather good at striking them for having such nubby fingers!" she explained, looking psychotic. "Teddy will finish the job for me in just a few minutes," she added, acting like she had won.

Arielle went to grab a bag of belongings off the counter.

I guess she forgot I smoked... she was so caught up in her own little world that she had forgotten that one thing...

If I'm going to die... I'm taking her with me. I don't have any other option...

I slowly grabbed the lighter from my pocket, making sure she didn't see me. Then I raised it high in the air...

"Hey Arielle..." I shouted sternly.

She turned back. "What do you want now?" Squinting at my hand, her eyes grew fearful.

"Haven't you ever heard of Samson?" I asked...

Then I sparked the lighter...

Epilogue
"It's Cold Out"
NARRATED BY ADAM
(Spring 2017)

I stand up and take a bow. "That's the end guys, that's all she wrote," I say yawning. It was getting late, the middle of the night. We had been outside around the fire for hours.

"That was awesome!" Tanya says excitedly.

"Yeah, great story!" Desiree adds, standing to her feet to stretch.

"That's it? That's how it ends?" Matt groans.

"It's definitely good," Eric interjects, finishing his beer, then throwing the bottle onto the ground.

"I just borrowed it," I say, laughing nervously.

We all watch the fire burning out... there isn't much of a flame left. The sky is clear now, and the moon is shining bright. I realize my shoes are getting wet from the dew.

"Matt, you want to help me set up these tents?" I ask. I had brought a tent, and Eric had lugged over his parents' giant, busted-up wigwam.

"Sure," he responds.

I hear a band of coyotes off in the distance. Sounds like they are feasting on some innocent creature. She won't admit it, but the sound makes Tanya change her mind about sleeping outside. She uses the weather as an excuse.

"Um... Adam," Tanya begins softly. "Can we crash at your place? It's getting really cold out."

"*Yeah* it is," Desiree agrees.

I think for a second. "Yeah, we can probably do that. Mom won't mind. I have two recliners, and a pull-out bed. You can all fight over who sleeps where."

"I call recliner!" Matt says.

Good call, I don't think that flimsy bed could support your ass...

"Okay well... we gotta clean up first," I say, picking up empty beer cans.

"I'll put out the fire," Eric announces, probably walking over to piss on it, like he always did. (I'm just glad I don't have to drag his drunk-ass home.)

I pick up a tent, still in its bag, and hoist it onto my shoulder. Eric and Matt grab the other tent and the folding chairs. The girls handle the bag of empties, then we head down the path to my house.

Sara trots up and wraps her arms around mine, trying to stay warm I assume. I don't mind, she is short and cute after all.

The stars gleam bright... like a million little

spotlights floating in space. The ground crunches under our feet, as we walk through loose stones. Crickets are still jamming their tune in every direction. I start walking faster, my legs feeling numb from the cold air.

We reach my stoop and set everything down to rest our arms. Then we stroll inside quietly. Everyone gathers in the living room and starts to settle down and warm up. Then Mom comes walking downstairs...

"Hey guys," she says cheerfully. "I heard you come in."

"We didn't wake you, did we?" I ask, feeling bad.

"No... no, it's not a problem," she says. "Does anyone want hot cocoa?" Everyone says yes.

Mom goes into the kitchen to make drinks...

"Dude... I hope it's okay to ask but..." Matt starts.

"My mom?" I ask.

He nods. "What happened to her? She's all..." He doesn't know how to finish his sentence.

I look down. All eyes on me now. Everyone is waiting for me to respond. *I feel like a circus clown...*

I hate having to explain why my mom looks so strange. Why she has second-degree and full thickness burns that cover her arms. I hate it when people stare at the skin grafts on her face... her blotchy, discolored skin.

Mom used to be beautiful. She showed me pictures from when she was a teen. She looked like a supermodel with the prettiest face and gorgeous, transparent red hair.

Now she wears a wig because most of her hair won't grow back. But she doesn't let any of that bother her anymore...

Mom says we are lucky to be alive... that I was in her belly when she was in the accident... when she got burned.

I never got to meet my real father. Mom told me he went missing and died the *same night* I was conceived... I almost never had a chance.

Yeah, okay... so you caught me.

I know the truth.

But of course, I will never admit it...

The Placebo Effect

A Multi-Narrative Horror/Thriller

Steve Wyffels

Made in the USA
Middletown, DE
09 September 2023